SHALOTT

In memory of Bonnie

I'm so grateful to my friends and writing colleagues as, without
them, I might never have finished Shalott. Special thanks to Elizabeth,
who understood my vision and gave me the courage to continue,
and to Linsay Knight for making it all happen. My thanks also
to Ruth, Eleanor and Kate for their input and encouragement;
to editors Catherine and Glenda for their excellent advice,
and to my husband Mike, who lives with my obsession and
who helped me follow the Arthurian trail.

Random House Australia Pty Ltd
20 Alfred Street, Milsons Point NSW 2061
http://www.randomhouse.com.au

Sydney New York Toronto
London Auckland Johannesburg
and agencies throughout the world

National Library of Australia
Cataloguing-in-Publication Data

Pulman, Felicity
Shallot.

ISBN 1 74 051727 X.

I. Title

A823.3

Photographs of the author by Mike Pulman.
Cover design by Monkeyfish.
Typeset by Asset Typesetting Pty Ltd in 13/17 Joanna.
Printed by Griffin Press Pty Ltd, Adelaide.

Shalott

felicity Pulman

RANDOM HOUSE AUSTRALIA

CHAPTER ONE

'Imagine you are in Camelot,' their teacher had said when she set Callie's class the assignment. 'What would you see? What would you do there?' To which Callie had silently added her own question: Could I change the story if I was part of it? Could I save Camelot?

There was only one way to find out.

Callie sat at her father's VR computer, staring at her reflection on the blank screen. Only an outline, frail and insubstantial, showed that she was there.

Maybe she wasn't really? Maybe she was a ghost?

She felt like one sometimes, drifting about on the

margins. Not like her twin sister, El, who lived life to the fullest and was involved in absolutely everything. Callie envied El. She wished she had El's certainty about her place in the world and the way she lived her life. It seemed to Callie that she was never sure of anything. Her lack of confidence paralysed her, left her dependent on her twin to tell her what to do.

Except for this assignment. It was an experiment, nothing to do with anyone else. Because this version was for her eyes only, which gave her the freedom to do exactly as she liked. Freedom. To Callie, the concept was both terrifying and exhilarating. She switched on the machine and, using her father's technology, she began to scan in the scenes she would need.

Virtual reality. Almost as real as the real thing. She would create Camelot. She would scan in the principal players of the legend: King Arthur and his wife, Guinevere. Her lover, Lancelot, the bravest knight in all the realm. Arthur's bastard son, Mordred. Merlin and Morgan le Fay, weavers of magic, would also be there. So would Arthur's followers, the knights of the Round Table who, at the end, had been forced to question their fidelity and every principle by which they lived. They would all be there, a potent mixture of personalities whose intrigues had brought about disgrace, despair and the bloody battle that had ended a kingdom.

But what role could she play? What could she do to alter the story and so save Camelot?

The key, she thought, was the illicit love affair between Guinevere and Lancelot, the liaison that had divided the court and left the way open for Mordred to work his poison.

She scanned a school photograph of herself onto the screen and made a few quick alterations. In place of her uniform, a long green silk gown, a gold necklet about her throat, a jewelled band for her hair.

She stared at her image on the screen. No longer a ghost. But not Callie either. Who, then? She looked as real as all the others at court. But did she have the power to change things, the power she lacked in real life? That was the question!

Perhaps she could use magic? But what sort? The old ways of the Celts? Pagan practices?

No! The knights had gone in search of the Holy Grail, the cup that had held Christ's blood. She was going to a Christian court, not a pagan one.

Except that Arthur was conceived because of Merlin's spell on his father, while Mordred's aunt, Morgan le Fay, used black magic to wreak havoc on the court, and on Arthur in particular. Pagan or Christian? It was impossible to tell. Callie came to the conclusion that any tricks she used would have to be of her own devising. Perhaps magic wasn't necessary after all. Perhaps all she needed was modern technology and a will to succeed.

Magic. The lines of Tennyson's poem came into Callie's mind: the one about the Lady of Shalott, the 'fairy' who weaved the 'mirror's magic sights', who was condemned to die should she ever look out the window at the real world.

Callie looked at her virtual self and at the world she had created on the computer. The Lady of Shalott had experienced her surroundings just as she, Callie, was doing now. Thoughtfully, she scanned a mirror onto the screen, placing its small, square frame on top of a chest of drawers. Its shiny surface reflected the world outside the tower, the world that the Lady could see only as shadows.

Callie and the Lady of Shalott. Twin souls, closer in spirit than Callie and her own twin sister. It made Callie feel less lonely to have a companion on the screen. 'What shall we do?' she whispered to her reflection. 'How shall we save Camelot?'

Callie felt a sudden flutter of excitement in her stomach as she recalled what their teacher had told them about the Lady of Shalott.

'It's thought that Tennyson based his poem and the Lady on Sir Thomas Malory's story of the Lily Maid, Elaine of Astolat, a young woman who fell in love with Lancelot and who killed herself when he would neither marry her nor take her for his mistress.'

The Lady of Shalott! Maybe *she* was the key to saving Camelot? Because, Callie thought, if I can make

Lancelot fall in love with me, then the Lady of Shalott won't have to die. Guinevere will stay faithful to King Arthur, and the court will unite behind Arthur to vanquish Mordred.

Simple, really. Except …

Except it hadn't happened then, so it wouldn't happen now … unless she, Callie, was prepared to change things, to make something happen. Like what?

She studied the image on the screen. With a shock of recognition, she realised what was wrong. Her lowered lids and shy expression distanced the Lady of Shalott from reality. This was the face of a dreamer, not a fighter. The Lady would need courage to change her destiny; courage and the will to enchant Lancelot, to make him forget Guinevere and fall in love with her instead. Callie picked up the mouse. Could she change the Lady's character by changing her expression?

The door flung open behind Callie and crashed against the wall. Elaine, her twin sister, bounced into the room and skidded to a stop, fanning herself against the heat.

'I might have known you'd be hiding in here!' she accused. 'I thought you weren't allowed in the workroom while Dad was away?'

'I'm just playing with something.' Callie dropped the mouse and leaned close to the screen, trying to shield the graphics from her sister's inquisitive gaze.

El walked across the room. 'He'll kill you if you

mess up the stuff he's experimenting on. You know how important it is.'

'It's just something silly, it's nothing to do with Dad's project.' But everything to do with my future, Callie added silently, acknowledging that if she could only make this work, she could prove to her father that her ideas weren't totally off the wall. If she could change the legend, then maybe she could change other things too. Like her father's mind. It was what Callie wanted more than anything, but there was no way she would share her plans with El.

She stood up and turned around, blocking the screen from her sister. 'I'll delete everything before Dad gets home from his trip,' she lied. 'He'll never know.'

'That you've been in here?' El surveyed her sister with a sceptical expression. Then she half-turned and shouted over her shoulder, 'Meg! I've found her! We're in Dad's workroom.' She leaned around Callie, nudging her aside. 'What's that supposed to be?'

'The Lady of Shalott. I've just finished our English assignment.' Callie knew El would keep on at her until she was given an answer. She supposed it was safe to admit that much.

'What an idiot!'

For a moment Callie thought the comment was directed at her, until El continued. 'She's such a loser. She should've run off with Lancelot instead of lying down in a boat and dying like that.' El leaned closer, looking at the scene in the tower. 'God, she looks just like you! She's got your expression and everything.'

'Who has?' Meg hesitated in the doorway, then stepped into the workroom.

'Quick! Don't let Honey in!' El rushed forward at the sound of an excited yelp. But she was too late. A golden labrador catapulted through the open door and launched herself at Callie in a frenzy of excited licks and wriggles.

'Poor Honey.' Callie bent over and grabbed the squirming dog. She walked across the room and pushed Honey outside, closing the door with a determined bang. She leaned against the door, folding her arms. 'I hate shutting her out,' she said, as a frantic scratching started outside, accompanied by a mournful howl.

'It would be a dead giveaway if Dad found dog hairs in here.'

Meg glanced curiously around the sterile workshop and the huge machine that dominated it. 'Is this where your dad researches his programs and things?'

'Yeah. I don't often get a chance to sneak in these days.' Callie moved swiftly, backing up against the screen to hide it from view. She wished they would go away. She'd been enjoying herself until their intrusion.

'Why won't your dad let you come in?'

'Cos he doesn't want Callie interfering with history,' El answered.

'Whatever do you mean?'

'El's exaggerating.' Callie cast a resentful glance at her sister. 'Dad's been doing some work for the Education Department on interactive history programs, where students can role-play famous scenes from history along with the characters who made it all happen.' And then, as Meg looked bewildered, she added, 'You know, you could be there to watch Cook landing in Australia, or King John signing the Magna Carta, or the Boston Tea Party in America.'

'Only Dad got cranky cos Callie kept wanting to change events, to see what would happen.' El giggled. 'That's why she's barred now.'

Callie felt her throat constrict. She swallowed down tears. Her questions had been innocent enough: What if the southerly hadn't blown Cook off course and some other country had colonised Australia? What if King John had refused to sign? What if Britain had managed to negotiate with America and they'd stayed part of the British Commonwealth? But her father's impatience had erupted into anger. And pain. Callie had seen the expression in his eyes as he'd roared, 'That's enough, Charlotte! You're just as impractical as your mother!' For a moment, he'd looked as if he hated her.

He'd apologised later, and told her he missed her visits to his workroom. But Callie knew her input wasn't wanted and so she hadn't gone back. Until now. Now, when she could answer her questions in her own way, without her father looking over her shoulder and criticising her. And if her idea worked, surely he'd have to take notice then?

'Dad's gone to an international conference to talk about the Virtual Humans program,' El said. 'I wonder if he'll talk about his new project?' she added unexpectedly.

'It's supposed to be a secret,' Callie warned.

El ignored her. 'He says if he can get his new idea off the ground, he'll be able to revolutionise the whole world.'

'Shut up, El. We're not supposed to say anything about it.'

'You can tell Meg. It's not as if she's a spy for ASIO!'

Meg laughed. 'I won't say a word, I swear.' She crossed her heart and leaned forward, studying the screen for clues. 'What's he doing?'

El shrugged. 'As well as all the historical stuff he's already got, he's trying to set up a whole lot of domestic and international scenarios for the future. But you'll have to ask Callie. I don't understand all this whizz-bang technology.'

'If there's a crisis somewhere, Dad plans to key in the major players and let them play through all the moves,' Callie explained reluctantly. 'I mean, say a foreign country like Indonesia became a threat to Australia in some way. Dad would factor everything into the program, and then set events in motion to find out what might happen. For instance, how many people would be killed if there was a war, or could the government negotiate a settlement. That sort of thing.'

'Surely you just need a good imagination to work it out?'

'Not necessarily. The computer will factor every possible variable into the program, so a whole lot of different scenarios are played out. In that way, the government can check out every option and look at all the repercussions. I mean, in this case Australia might respond with a team of mediators instead of troops, or promise more aid or whatever. It's supposed to take the risk out of decision making, because the outcome of any decision would be more certain.'

'Sounds fantastic! Is the program up and running yet?'

'Not yet. And it's really secret, so you mustn't talk about it.' Callie's fingers caressed the keyboard. She itched to be left in peace.

'So are you trying to work out some stuff for your dad while he's away?' Meg asked shrewdly.

'No!' Callie wondered how to satisfy Meg's curiosity without betraying her own plans. 'I'm just fooling around with some graphics.'

'Dad can't stand it when she gets all arty.' El laughed. 'He's always nagging Callie to pull herself together and come down to earth. He says she spends most of her time lost in space.'

'And what do you say?' Meg asked.

'I don't say anything. It's hard to argue with Dad. He wants me to be more like El. More switched on, more practical. But I can't. Even though we're twins, we're quite different. He can't seem to understand that.'

Callie glanced resentfully at her sister, knowing their difference was something El also found hard to understand, or accept. Making a deliberate effort to seem calm she reached up, yawning elaborately, stretching her cramped arms and back.

'It's more than that. It's because you're artistic, like our mother. He hates it that you're so like her.'

Callie flinched, unable to defend herself against El's cheerful cruelty. El and Dad hardly ever mentioned their mother, but Callie missed her. As soon as she'd seen how Callie loved to experiment with the paints in her studio, her mother had given Callie a large box of paints of her own. She had shown her how to draw, to paint, to experiment with colour. If only Callie could talk to her father like she might have talked to her mother. If only she could tell him about her hopes, her dreams for the future. She had tried once, but he had cut her off. 'Pull yourself together, Callie. You sound just like your mother when you talk like that. She couldn't deal with reality either.'

Callie had stuttered into silence and gone off to her room. Seizing a block of paper, she had sketched her mother's face, so well-remembered even though she'd been gone for nearly six years. As the face came to life under her fingers, Callie had found herself crying and cursing. She wondered if the pain would ever go away as, with shaking fingers, she had ripped the sketch into tiny pieces.

'Can't you get your mum on side? Can't she help you change your dad's mind?'

'We don't even know where she is,' El answered.

'But one of these days I might go and look for her.' Callie put her dream into words.

'Dad would never let you!'

'I can see why you enjoy playing with this.' Meg felt sorry for Callie as she watched her turn away, trying to hide her misery. She wished she could get to know her better. Callie could do with a friend. But Callie was reserved, shy. And El was always there to speak for her. Meg tapped the screen. 'That girl looks even more like you than El does,' she observed.

'The Lady of Shalott?'

'Is that who you were drawing?' Meg tilted her head, assessing the figure and its reflection in the mirror. 'But it's you, isn't it? You've put yourself in the tower.'

'Yes.'

'And I can see why. I mean, I don't say you're going to die for love or anything stupid like that,' Meg added quickly as she noticed Callie's frown, 'but you have to admit you have something in common with her.'

El strolled over, her gaze moving from the screen to

her sister. 'Meg's right. I never thought of it before, but you're just like the Lady of Shalott.'

'I am not!'

'Yes you are.' El traced the outline of the figure on the screen. 'Come on, admit you don't have a life either. When you're not at school you mope around in your room drawing or painting. Now you're not helping Dad set up his programs, you spend all your spare time on your own. You never hang out with us at all. Does she, Meg?' She turned to her friend and Meg nodded. 'Like now,' El continued. 'We were looking for you to see if you want to come down to the mall with us, to check out the sales. But I bet you say no.'

Callie sighed. She wished El would back off, would respect the differences between them and give her some space.

'You're right. I'll say no,' she agreed, hoping that they would take the hint and go away.

'But I can see why you want to stay and work on this.' Meg said again, trying to defuse the tension between the sisters. 'It looks so real!' She smiled at Callie. 'I wish you could do my assignment. I don't even know which poem to choose. All that old poetry is so boring.'

'Boring?' Callie shook her head, trying to understand. 'How can you say that? I mean, look at the Lady of Shalott. She spends all her life locked in a tower, spinning out the scenes reflected in her mirror, then when she finally catches sight of Lancelot and falls in love with him, she dies. It's tragic!'

'Maybe we can do something about that?' With a grin, El picked up the mouse and drew a large square shape beside the figure in the tower.

'What are you doing?' Callie snatched the mouse and hurriedly erased the clumsy drawing.

'Giving her a jukebox. She could have a party up there.' El giggled. 'We could draw some guys for her to dance with.'

'What a great idea!' cried Meg.

Callie's grip tightened on the mouse. 'She's supposed to be alone.'

'Where does it say that in the poem?' Meg picked up the book that lay on the stand beside Callie and held it out. Her gaze moved from Callie to the young woman on the screen. 'She does look lonely,' she said, observing the shy, downcast expression.

'Draw us in with her,' El demanded. 'I want to see myself up there with you.'

Callie's mouth tightened into a thin angry line. She'd set herself this task as an experiment, to try something out. If it worked, it would prove her talent to her father; prove that whatever he might think, there was some practical application for her artistic ability. His trip overseas had been an unexpected bonus. She didn't want to waste precious time fooling around. There was so much more at stake here than she was willing to confess. Exasperated, she turned on her sister. 'It would take too long to draw you in. I need a photograph.'

'I bet you've got one here.' El riffled through the pile of books and papers on a shelf beside Callie. 'Thought so!' She pulled out a photo and waved it above her head. It was one of a series taken of the twins for their grandmother's birthday. She handed it to her sister to be scanned, and turned to Meg. 'What about you?'

'I think I've still got those pix we took at the booth outside Woolies last week.' Meg pulled out a bulging wallet and rummaged through the stack of papers crammed into it. 'Here they are!' She held out a strip of photographs.

Recognising defeat, Callie scanned the two images, placing her sister and Meg beside the lady in the tower. Maybe when they'd admired themselves, they'd get sick of the whole thing and go away.

'I want a red dress, long, embroidered with gold and pearls,' El instructed. 'And a gold girdle and purse like you've got. And I want rubies and pearls around my throat, and rings and things.' She gave the green-robed figure a disparaging look. 'You should give her a bit more jewellery too. Those lords and ladies used to dress up in the Middle Ages.'

'You'd know, of course,' Callie grumbled as her fingers tap-danced over the keys, filling in colours.

El tossed her head. 'I saw the movie.'

'*First Knight?*' Callie snorted with laughter. 'That's the Hollywood version. It's nothing like the real story. At the end of the real story, Lancelot goes into exile, Guinevere joins a convent, and Arthur and Mordred kill each other at the Battle of Camlann.'

'Whatever.' El wasn't interested. 'Look.' She pointed at an illustration in the book lying open beside Callie. 'They're all dressed up.' She picked it up and inspected the cover. '*Morte d'Arthur* by Sir Thomas Malory.' She pulled a face at Callie. 'Surely we don't have to read all this stuff as well?'

'No, we don't. But I'm interested in the story.' Callie grabbed the book from El and hugged it to her chest.

'So give me the sort of jewellery they're wearing.'

'Have it your own way.' Callie checked the illustration and got busy. She knew from long experience that her sister would keep on at her until she'd got what she wanted. So the quicker Callie could finish, the sooner she'd be left in peace. 'What about your hair?'

'Do it like yours. It's quite nice.' El's fingers touched her own hair. It was dark and wavy, like Callie's, but braided neatly in a French plait. 'I mean the way you've done it on the screen. Do mine like that.' She smiled with pleasure at the image coming to life before her, not noticing the small, subtle differences. Perhaps Callie hadn't intended them, might not have been conscious of re-creating them, but they were there in the broad swimmer's shoulders and muscular stance, and the bold, confident, twenty-first century eyes.

'What about you, Meg?' Callie turned an inquiring glance on her friend. More El's friend than hers, really. Her mouth tightened in a small grimace of acceptance as she acknowledged the truth of El's accusation that she didn't have much of a life outside school.

But I like it this way, she reassured herself. She looked at the scanned image on the screen: the slight frame and quizzical expression of her sister's friend. 'I'll have to give you long hair,' she said, lengthening the cropped hairstyle, stroking the dark hair straight and long down Meg's back. 'And I'd better take the ring out of your nose.' She placed a gold circlet around Meg's forehead, set with jewels, then dressed her in a gown of peacock blue with a gold, embroidered trim. 'What do you think?'

'Very fine.' Meg smiled in satisfaction. 'I look quite the lady, don't I?' She pirouetted, then sank low in a curtsey.

El giggled as she glanced at Meg's faded jeans and old T-shirt. 'It's a bit more up-market than the ratty gear you usually wear.'

Meg wobbled, then straightened hurriedly. 'Clothes don't matter. It's what's inside that counts,' she snapped, then added defensively, 'Anyway, I don't get a big allowance like you two.'

'Scroll through the rest of it. What else have you done?' Oblivious of Meg's resentment, El pointed to the control panel in front of Callie.

Annoyed with her sister and her big mouth and wanting to divert attention from Meg, Callie moved from the computer screen to the large machine beside it. 'Grab some goggles and gloves,' she said, as she pulled on her own equipment. She stepped up onto a platform and faced a panel of instruments.

'This looks like something from *Star Wars*,' Meg observed, as Callie's fingers played across the complicated array of knobs and dials.

'Except we're going back in time, not forward.' Callie flicked a switch to activate the motion platform.

'So you've actually created the world of King Arthur and the knights of the Round Table?' Meg asked as they descended stone stairs and left the tower.

'Not all of it. This is all stuff I've scanned in from Dad's history program, but I've still got to put in the characters and everything.'

'Well, we look the part.' Meg glanced sideways at Callie in her green dress. 'We look just like you've drawn us.'

'Yeah.' El laughed. 'And we're not even wearing goggles. We look really medieval.'

'So where's Camelot then?' Meg asked as the path took a bend through meadows starred with yellow and white daisies. They were approaching the bank of a river now. Glints of sunlight on water marked its passage through a girdle of green trees.

'Over there!' Callie pointed towards the stone walls of a settlement that nestled at the base of a fortified castle. In the distance, fields of ripening crops stood golden under a blazing sky.

'On either side the river lie
Long fields of barley and of rye,
That clothe the wold and meet the sky;
And thro' the field the road runs by
  To many-towered Camelot …'

Callie sang the words softly under her breath as the scene unfurled in front of them. 'I've tried to design it as Tennyson's poem described it. The tower is behind us now, and Camelot's down the river. No-one knows where it really was, so I'm just making it up as I go along.'

The road looped down, skirting the green forest to run parallel with the dark, shining river that swung now into the open. It was framed by the hanging fronds of weeping willows and formed a natural boundary for one side of the walled settlement. Meg and El watched, fascinated, as the road looped once more, curving back towards the heavy iron gates that marked the main entrance.

'Take us into Camelot,' said El. Callie pressed a

button. The gates lifted to let them through and then banged down again behind them. They travelled past reed-thatched huts of wattle and daub, small dwellings that became larger and more prosperous-looking as they approached the town square. Dominating the skyline were the stone walls of the castle. Flags flew from the turrets, but the stronghold seemed deserted.

'Arthur's court,' Meg announced with satisfaction as they climbed up to it. 'Have you drawn him in with Guinevere yet?'

'This is all I've done so far.' Callie's sensitive touch opened huge doors of carved oak that led them through to a corridor bordering a courtyard. Roses perfumed the air, while flower-filled gardens set brilliant splashes of colour against the grey stone flagging. 'Through here,' Callie directed as she guided them into an antechamber. A short, wide flight of stone stairs took them up to the Great Hall. It was empty.

Bright embroidered tapestries depicting hunting scenes decorated the walls. These were positioned between sconces which at night held flaming torches to illuminate them. By day the torches were unlit and the room was dark and gloomy.

'I haven't had time to put in a lot of detail.'

'Dad doesn't get home until next weekend. Will you take us on a tour of the whole thing when you've got it done?'

'If you like.' Callie pulled off her goggles, sure now

that they would leave her in peace. She smiled at them and waggled her fingers. Goodbye.

'But we'll just fix up the lady in the tower before we go.' El had read her sister's mind. 'And you're not to rub us out after we leave, Callie. We'll put some guys in the tower with us. If she could have just partied on in her room, I reckon the Lady would never have fallen for Lancelot and she might not have had to die.'

'What?' Callie was startled that her sister's thoughts seemed to be running parallel to her own. Almost. But she was trying to re-create the poem with her own subtle variations, not El's. If it worked, the variations would change the legend but, more importantly, it would show her father what she, and the program, could do. She certainly wasn't interested in messing things up for her sister's sake.

'Go back, Callie. We're going to change the legend,' El announced.

Callie felt a moment's panic. 'No!' She crossed her fingers behind her back. 'I'll do it later.'

'Now!' El commanded. 'Take us back to the tower.' And then, as Callie still made no move, she reached out to the panel of instruments. 'Come on!'

'No!' Callie brushed El's arm away.

El smiled in satisfaction as she watched her reluctant sister retrace their steps. 'Okay, now put some guys in,' she said, as their figures appeared in the tower once more. 'You can start with ...'

'Lancelot!' cried Meg. 'Draw Lancelot in the room, then the Lady won't have to look out the window at him.' She pulled off her goggles and gloves and slung them onto a hook, adding El's and Callie's as they handed them over.

'That might be fun.' El stepped down from the motion platform and pushed her sister in the direction of the computer. 'Go on, Callie. Scan him in. I know there's a picture of him in our poetry book.' Once more she scratched through Callie's pile of references. 'Here.' She pulled it out. Before she had time to search, the pages fell open to the place she wanted: a much-thumbed portrait of Lancelot astride his horse, silvery armour gleaming in the sunlight. She read the stanza beside it:

'His broad clear brow in sunlight glowed;
On burnished hooves his war-horse trode;
From underneath his helmet flow'd
His coal-black curls as on he rode,
    As he rode down to Camelot.'

Callie sat down. Her fingers moved over the controls, bringing the image of Lancelot to the screen: the perfect knight who was part of her plan. She knew his features by heart. She was half in love with him already.

'Ooh-er! Not bad!' El nudged Meg. 'I wouldn't mind getting on with him.'

'He's probably boring.' Meg checked out the tall, handsome figure with its pious expression.

'Boring?' Callie flashed to the defence of her imaginary hero. 'He's the most tragic figure of them all. He was the one caught in the middle: caught between his love for Guinevere and his loyalty and duty to Arthur. Even though he was the best and bravest knight in Arthur's court, because he had an affair with Guinevere he was judged unworthy to find the Holy Grail. In the end, his guilt drove him mad.'

'So why did the Lady of Shalott die for him if he was already in love with Guinevere?'

'I guess she didn't know that the bimbo queen was her rival.' El turned to Callie. 'But Meg's right. If Lancelot gets together with Guinevere at the end, he's no good for the Lady of Shalott. We need someone who'll fall in love with her and save her.'

'But the Lady's supposed to fall in love with Lancelot. That's part of the legend,' Callie protested.

'And we're going to change it. So you have to find someone else.' El seized the mouse and clicked, deleting the figure before Callie had a chance to protest.

Callie glared at her sister. 'I was enjoying myself until you came,' she said pointedly. She snatched the mouse back from El, mourning the loss of the knight who had captured her imagination and who held the key to her future.

'We're not going until we've found some guys to

keep us company.' El sounded determined. Head tilted, she stared out of the window at the sunshine leaching from the golden afternoon. 'You can try and draw Greg for me while we're thinking who else to put in,' she instructed as she walked towards the door and snapped on the lights.

'He's your boyfriend. That's also boring,' Meg objected. 'Let's have characters we don't know, really off-the-wall guys so we can have some fun. Oh, I know!' She grabbed the mouse from Callie and sat down beside her on the bench.

'Be careful! Make sure you don't hit that green switch.' Callie moved quickly, pushing herself in front of the controls to protect them.

'What happens if you do?' Meg asked, casting a fascinated glance at the control panel.

'You save everything. And that's the last thing I want.' Once more, Callie crossed her fingers behind her back, to cancel out the lie. 'I don't want Dad to know I've been in here. He'll think I've been experimenting with his new project.'

'Aren't you frightened you'll screw it up?'

'No. I know what I'm doing.'

'You hope!' scoffed El.

'What happens if you push this?' Meg pointed to a red button. 'Can we play a game or something?'

'No!' Callie swiped Meg's hand away. 'Don't touch anything.'

'Can I just draw on the screen then?' Without waiting for permission, Meg pointed the mouse and drew a shaky line.

'Who's that supposed to be?' In spite of her annoyance, Callie found herself smiling at the stick figure emerging from Meg's unskilled hand.

'That cute new guy in our history class. You know, with the dreadlocks?' Thin scratchings erupted from around the outline of the head, so that it looked like a child's drawing of the sun. 'Damn,' Meg muttered as she erased the head and tried again.

'That's not fair! We weren't allowed to have the guys we wanted, so why should you?' El protested.

'Well ...' Meg shrugged. 'I guess we'd better think about who we do want, then.' She glanced at her watch and leapt to her feet. 'I've got to go,' she said, heading towards the door at speed. 'It's church tonight.'

'Why do you bother?' El asked. 'Surely you don't go for all that goody-goody Christian stuff?'

'I like going.' Meg looked a little embarrassed. 'Actually, they've asked me to join the band. We play some really good music. I get to sing, too.'

'Well, that's great,' Callie encouraged her. 'You're really good at playing the guitar, and you've got an ace voice. I don't know how you remember songs so quickly.'

'I like music.' Meg hesitated, wondering if it was possible to explain to her friends that music gave her the same joyous feeling of reverence as looking up at the dark vault of a starry sky, or watching waves crashing against pink sandstone cliffs. Music threaded through her days and through her dreams at night. It was part of her life.

She sighed. Callie might understand. El never would. And she didn't have time to explain anyway. 'Why don't you come and listen to us sometime?' she said, instead. 'The Pentecostal church is nothing like that old Sunday school thing. It's theatre. It's fun.'

'Can't today, thanks.' El straightened up from the computer. 'I promised Gran I'd cook tea. She's off at her bridge club this afternoon.' She turned to Callie. 'Save it,' she said. 'We'll do some more work on it tomorrow.'

'Can I come over and watch?' Meg paused, her hand on the door handle.

'Of course,' El answered for Callie. 'Just have a think about who you want to include. We'll each nominate someone.'

'I don't want anyone else,' Callie argued. 'The Lady of Shalott is supposed to be alone. You're spoiling it, El.'

'Rubbish!' El gave her a friendly push. 'Come over after school,' she told Meg. 'We'll wait for you.'

'I won't be here.' Callie folded her arms and glared at them both.

'Then we'll just have to start without you.'

Callie swore under her breath. El knew nothing

about the program, or how to get into it, but she knew her sister well enough to know that El wouldn't give up that easily.

Meg's sympathy was with Callie. Why didn't she ever stand up for herself? But Callie was a dreamer, while El always knew exactly what she wanted. It was hard to go against El once she'd made up her mind. Meg wished she could think of something to get Callie on side. Then she had an inspiration.

'I know!' she cried. 'My mum's got a Polaroid. I'll bring it to school tomorrow. We can choose some guys and photograph them!'

'Fantastic!' El turned to Callie. 'That'll make it easier for you to scan them in,' she said, nudging her playfully.

Furious, Callie pulled away. 'I'll lock up. You can get going.' Despite El's warning, once she was alone she intended to delete everything.

'We're not going till you've saved it all.' El stepped close to Callie, standing over her. For a moment they stood toe to toe, both defiant, each determined to have her own way. El's hand moved towards the control panel.

Callie felt like screaming. A hot wave of anger pulsed through her body and her hands clenched into fists. With a savage swipe, she pushed her sister out of the way and set about saving the program. What if her father found traces of El's silly fantasy later? This wasn't how she'd planned things at all. 'Okay, I've done it. Are you satisfied now?' She leaned against the computer, waiting for them to leave. With an apologetic glance, Meg opened the door. There was an excited yelp. They'd forgotten Honey.

The dog raced inside, then stopped abruptly and set up a furious scratching. El bent and scooped Honey up in her arms.

'Honey needs a bath,' she observed. 'She's full of fleas and she's beginning to pong.'

Angry and resentful, Callie walked with them to the door and watched them leave. Meg paused for a moment to fondle Honey's ears before hurrying next door to get ready for church. El dawdled behind her, hugging Honey. The dog licked her face and squirmed to get free.

It was almost dark. Callie felt her hair crinkle with electricity as she breathed in the hot, dry air. There was a strong smell of smoke. Bushfires. Several new outbreaks had been reported on the morning news. Firefighters were on full alert. She looked up at the sky. It seemed to hang just over her head, belly-heavy with smoke and tinged with the fierce red of the fiery ring that surrounded the city. Still too far away to worry about, but nowhere was really safe in the bushfire season.

A ring of fire ...

Something cold squeezed Callie's heart. With a quick intake of breath, she stumbled inside and switched off the computer. The machine hissed gently. The lighted screen dwindled to a small glowing eye as medieval time gave way to the twenty-first century.

With a sigh of angry frustration, Callie snapped off the lights and walked out, locking the door behind her. Somehow she had to deflect El's and Meg's interest in her work; somehow she had to get them off her back. Her father would be home soon enough. She really couldn't afford to waste any more time. But she'd have to come up with something really good to put El off. She knew her sister too well to suppose that she might do as Callie asked, and leave her alone. It just wasn't El's way.

CHAPTER TWO

'Check that! I haven't seen him before.' Meg nudged El as a tall guy in the uniform of St John's College climbed onto the bus and walked down the aisle towards them. She scratched through her bag, scattering its contents across the aisle and under the seats in her hurry. She whipped out her camera, squinted through the lens and captured him on film.

Startled, he paused and glanced at her. A faint smile twitched the corners of his mouth. He smoothed back already smooth fair hair as he turned and slotted into the seat in front of them, fanning himself with one hand. The hair at the back of his neck, regulation short above the white collar, was dark with sweat. Callie wondered why he didn't take off his blazer. But the St John's guys never did, no matter how high the temperature climbed. Better to burn than break the rules. She slouched back in her seat, glad of her thin cotton uniform with its short sleeves.

'Wow!' Meg breathed. 'Who is he?'

'Who knows. Who cares.' El shrugged. Her attention was focused on the passengers pushing onto the bus. 'Greg's late,' she muttered, craning around to scan several students still waiting on the pavement.

'Maybe he got a lift to school?' Meg scuffled around on the floor for her possessions and stuffed them back into her schoolbag. Then she picked up the camera and studied the photograph with satisfaction.

'He didn't say anything on the phone last night about getting a lift.'

Callie sat quietly, letting the talk flow past her. She was trying to become invisible, hoping that El and Meg might forget about her and make other arrangements for the afternoon, so that she could return to Camelot in peace.

'Wake up, Callie.' Meg waved the photograph under her nose. 'What do you think? Is he your type?'

'No.' Callie didn't care if the guy heard her. But he had pulled out a mobile phone and was busy punching in a number. He wasn't paying any attention to them.

'No-one this century is Callie's type,' El joked. 'She's after the perfect knight, remember? We'll have to —'

'Tony! Mate!' A loud voice cut across their conversation. 'Yeah, I'm on the bus. Can you believe it? I had to take the car in yesterday. Air con. I told them they've got till today to fix it. I need that cool, man.'

There was a brief silence. Meg looked at the photograph as if debating whether or not to rip it up. But then she thrust it into a fat textbook to keep it safe.

'Yeah, I got the notes you wanted. I'll give them to you at recess. No problem.' The guy clicked off the mobile and lounged back in his seat. El poked a finger into her open mouth, miming vomiting.

Meg smiled. Callie paid no attention. She was seething with anger and disappointment as she came to terms with the fact that her sister and Meg would be waiting to sabotage her program again this afternoon.

Two guys walked up the aisle towards them. Callie recognised them. They were on the bus every day and they wore the same St John's uniform as the guy with the mobile. They stopped short when they saw him, then retreated a few steps.

'Mark! Jase!' The loud voice rang out once more. 'Over here!' He beckoned them down the bus.

'Stephen.' One of the newcomers flipped up a hand in acknowledgment. He looked around, then turned and followed his mate to a seat near the front, behind the driver.

'Mr Unpopular,' El commented loudly. The guy in front of them swivelled and gave her a filthy look. Then he turned back and began to punch another number into his mobile. They watched his ears stain pink. El smirked.

'Eddie! Mate! Did you have a good night?' The guy's voice cut across the growl of conversation as the bus filled up. With a whistle of compressing air, the doors swung shut. Gears ground, explosions of black smoke marked their passage as the bus jerked away from the pavement. Passengers who hadn't found seats gripped onto any handhold they could as they staggered down the aisle. A young girl paused beside the St John guy. Grudgingly, he shifted to make room for her, still talking. 'The best, mate! Yeah, I went to the club. Fake ID. You should've seen the babes. Too bad you couldn't come. Didn't get to bed till after three.' A loud laugh. 'Dunno why I'm going to school actually.'

'Dunno either.' El rolled her eyes and turned to Meg. 'Greg's not on the bus,' she added.

'Yeah, I noticed. But you'll see him at recess. Oh, look!' She nudged El. 'There's that cute new guy!' She picked up the camera. 'Love the hairstyle,' she murmured as she focused and clicked.

'Don't get any ideas,' El warned. 'You're not having him at Camelot. Not if I can't have Greg.'

'We'll see about that.' Meg waved the photograph in

the air to dry it before slipping it carefully into the textbook.

Callie sighed. 'Listen,' she said, 'you don't have to come this afternoon.' Desperation made her inventive. 'Give me a bunch of the photos and I'll choose. You can come and look when I've finished. It'll be a surprise.'

It would be a surprise, all right. She would get on and do what she wanted. Then she would explain to Meg and El that the computer had crashed and that she'd lost everything she'd saved. That way they wouldn't see what she was up to. And she would have the satisfaction of re-creating the legend the way she wanted. Because part of her plan was born out of pity for the tormented Sir Lancelot, and the guilty love he'd had for his queen — a guilt that had driven him to madness and helped to bring about the end of an empire. She wanted to change all that.

What, Callie asked herself, might have happened if Lancelot had truly fallen in love with the Lily Maid, Elaine of Astolat? Guinevere would have stayed faithful to King Arthur. And Elaine, the Lady of Shalott, would not have committed suicide.

She moved on then to the question that haunted her, the question she kept coming back to ever since she'd first read the poem and started her research on King Arthur and the Knights of the Round Table: if Lancelot hadn't betrayed Arthur with Guinevere, if he'd stayed to help Arthur fight Mordred for the Kingdom of Logres, could Camelot have been saved?

Callie was jerked from her dream as El laughed and gave her a hard jab in the ribs. 'If we leave everything to you, the whole place will be full of macho knights jousting and showing off their fighting skills while the ladies wring their hands and swoon in admiration. That's not my idea at all. I want your lady to have fun, not go off and kill herself like in that silly old legend. No, we'll be there right after school to make sure you give her a good time.'

'Dave! Mate!' The conversation from the seat in front started up again.

El groaned and clapped her hands over her ears. She sank lower, propping her knees against the seat in front, kicking it with her feet. 'What a retard,' she said loudly, her words ringing out over the monologue, momentarily silencing everyone on the bus.

The ears in front went pink again. But the phone calls were still going as the three of them climbed off the bus.

'Greg! Where were you? How did you get to school?' El pushed her way through the crowd thronging off the bus, and raced over to a muscular guy with sun-streaked hair.

'Wish I had someone cute like Greg for a boyfriend,' said Meg as she and Callie hoisted their bags over their shoulders and followed slowly.

'Heaps of guys want to go out with you,' said Callie, wishing she could make the same claim.

'Yeah, well.' Meg shrugged. 'It's hard to get excited about going out with guys you've known since they were zit-covered losers in Year Seven.'

'We were no different,' Callie pointed out.

'Yeah, but girls change. Guys just get bigger.' Meg's face brightened as the guy with dreadlocks brushed past them. 'So, how are you settling in, then?' she asked, quickening her pace to fall into step with him.

Callie pulled a face behind their backs. But she couldn't help feeling envious. She wished she had someone to talk to, someone she trusted enough to tell about her experiment with her dad's computer. It would be great to have someone who understood her plans, and who really cared what happened to her. She shifted her heavy bag onto her other shoulder and trailed dispiritedly after Meg.

A buzzer shrilled across the playground. Callie quickened her pace, passing a thin, shambling figure in stained jeans and torn shirt. Lev. She remembered his name from the few times he'd come to class. He didn't often bother.

'There's the bell. You'd better hurry,' she called over her shoulder. He stared at her, his face blank.

'It's English, first period. We're doing Tennyson.'

The guy didn't move. He seemed to be waiting for an explanation.

'It's important. It's part of our assessment for the HSC.' Callie walked back to him, wrinkling her nose at the smell of unwashed clothes and sweat. She wondered why Lev bothered to come to school at all.

'Uh … where do we have to go?' His words sounded slurred. She wondered if he was on something. Surely he couldn't be drunk at nine in the morning?

'I'll show you.' As she walked on, she realised he wasn't following her. 'Come on!' she called impatiently. 'We're late.'

He jerked into action, shambling after her with long, uneven strides.

'So, how've you been?' she asked, thinking she couldn't care less, yet unable to shake off a sharp stab of pity at his appearance. Did the guy sleep in a drain, or what?

'Oh. Okay. You know.'

Callie didn't, but didn't like to ask. She wondered about Lev and his lifestyle, but told herself it was none of her business.

'I haven't seen you for a while. How come you're at school today?' she found herself asking.

He glanced at her sideways, suspicion in his eyes. 'Nuthin' else to do.' He pulled his black woollen beanie down, jamming his ears inside it. He shivered then, in spite of the heat, and wrapped his arms around his thin frame. Callie stared at him curiously. There was a streak of dirt across his face; the skin underneath was an unhealthy, unwashed grey.

'Do you live near here? Near the school?' The corridors were almost empty now, but her steps had slowed in her curiosity to find out more.

Lev shrugged and wiped his nose on the back of his hand. He seemed unaware of his surroundings. His eyes stayed fixed on his shoes. Reeboks. New. How could he afford them, especially when the rest of him was so scruffy? He walked behind her, almost as if he was being towed.

'Do your olds live near here?' She tried again.

'Olds?' He laughed, a brief croak of sound that held no humour. 'Whaddya mean?'

Callie stopped dead. 'Your parents?' And then, as Lev stayed silent, 'Don't you have anyone to look after you?'

'Nuh.' Lev considered. 'There's me grandma, but she don't care. I look after meself.' He thrust his hands deep into his pockets and slouched after Callie as she set off again.

'Do you live with your grandma?'

'Nuh.' He didn't elaborate.

I was right, she thought. He does live in a drain. She touched Lev's arm, hating how he shrank away from her. 'In here,' she said, and led the way into the classroom.

'You're late.' Ms Hope pushed up her glasses and glared at them. Her eyes widened as she took in Lev's dishevelled appearance. 'There's a spare desk down there,' she said uncertainly, waving a hand towards the back of the room. 'Are you new to the school?'

'Nuh.' Lev slouched past the desks and banged into the spare seat. He had no books with him. His faded grey canvas backpack looked almost empty.

Ms Hope pulled her glasses off and fiddled with them as she watched Lev. Callie could sense her determination to get him off to the school counsellor as soon as the period was over. Ms Hope was young and keen. Callie wished her lots of luck. No matter how fierce Lev's protests of independence, it was clear he needed help.

She glanced at El's open book on the desk beside hers, then turned to the same place in her own. Not the Lady of Shalott today. She was glad of that. With luck, El and Meg might still forget their plans for the afternoon.

'The age that Tennyson was writing about is known as the age of chivalry,' said Ms Hope, raising her voice and banging her fist on the desk a couple of times to get their attention. 'Tennyson's poems are based on Sir Thomas Malory's book *Morte d'Arthur*, which tells of the adventures of King Arthur and the Knights of the Round Table: their battles against mythical monsters, their search for the Holy Grail, and the intrigues of the court, including the forbidden love between Guinevere and Lancelot.'

She pushed her glasses back into position and consulted the notes scribbled on a pad in front of her. 'An important part of the legend tells of the conflict between Mordred and Arthur. Mordred was Arthur's own son, born of an incestuous alliance between the king and his half-sister, Morgause. Mordred believed he was King Arthur's rightful heir and so he challenged Arthur for the Kingdom of Logres. They met at Camlann to discuss his claim, but one of the soldiers drew his sword to kill a snake that had bitten him. Unfortunately, a drawn sword was the signal to end the truce. The deaths of both Mordred and Arthur at the Battle of Camlann brought to an end — almost by accident — the legendary court of Camelot.'

Ms Hope's gaze travelled the classroom, her eyes resting on Callie who sat, upright and attentive, following every word of a story she already knew well. She smiled slightly, knowing Callie shared her passion for the legend. Her smile slipped as she noticed El sprawled next to her.

'Sit up and listen to me!' she snapped, smacking her hands together to wake up the rest of the class. 'You may need this information for your assignment.' She clenched and unclenched her fingers as she waited for everyone to look at her.

'But the end of Camelot probably started with the

search for the Holy Grail. It set friend against friend, brother against brother and killed many of Camelot's best knights. This truly Christian quest was a medieval addition to the earlier legends, and forms an interesting contrast to the high magic practised by Merlin, Nimue and Morgan le Fay. In fact, it's a reflection of what actually happened in Britain at the time of Roman occupation, when Christianity was grafted onto the much older pagan beliefs, which are the genesis of the Arthurian legend.'

'Boring.' Callie heard the mutter from behind, heard the soft scuffling of restless feet and the faint rustle of paper as a page was turned. A guy sitting at the back had a magazine on his lap and was drooling over pictures of half-naked women. Lev slumped beside him, his head resting on his folded arms on the desk. He seemed to be asleep.

'Essentially, the legend of King Arthur and the knights of the Round Table remains popular because it reflects the timeless struggle between high ideals and human nature. It challenges what we believe about our society and about ourselves, calling into question our personal notions of faith, honour, duty and courage.' Ms Hope picked up the book of poetry and cradled it in her hands. 'Like Arthur in his pursuit of a perfect society, we too should try to understand our world and find meaning in our lives and in the way that we live them. Only then can we hope to reach our full potential.'

Callie slumped back in her seat. She wasn't interested in the meaning of life. She was much more interested in the virtual world she'd created, and the knight who waited for her there.

Impatient now, she glanced at her watch and willed the time to pass. She must try again to persuade El and Meg not to interfere. Then, with a bit of luck, she could start changing the legend right away.

chapter three

'Okay Callie, let's go.' Callie had dawdled after school, deliberately missing the first bus. But El and Meg were waiting for her when she got home. There was no chance of escape. No chance of excuses either.

'Now, don't argue.' El grabbed her arm and propelled her down the path. 'We're coming to make sure you do it right.'

'Do it your way, you mean.' Callie's steps dragged but her mind raced as she tried to come up with an excuse, any good reason, not to do what El wanted. She couldn't think of a thing. At least, nothing that would convince her pig-headed sister anyway.

'What are the numbers?' El stopped at the door of the workroom and took hold of the combination lock.

'I forget.'

'Don't be silly, Callie. You remembered yesterday. What is it? Dad's birthday or something?'

'No. He wouldn't choose anything so obvious.'

'So what did he choose?' El waited. 'Dad's hopeless with numbers. It'd be something pretty easy to remember,' she prompted, as Callie stayed obstinately silent. 'Our birthday?' Her fingers twirled busily, but the lock didn't spring.

'The fires are getting worse,' Meg commented. The sky was prematurely dark, the air thick with bitter smoke. Flakes of ash and grit swirled around them. A hot wind lifted their hair and swirled their skirts; it fanned the fires and brought no cooling relief.

El grunted, still preoccupied with cracking the code. 'Help me, Callie! Is it Gran's birthday?'

But Callie too was looking at the sky and at the red circle that ringed the city.

'We've got a good view up here.' Meg swung around, suddenly anxious. 'Do you think we're in any danger?'

'Not yet. They're still quite far away. Anyway, there's a creek between us and the bush.' Callie frowned as she felt the same cold clutch of fear. Fire. A ring of fire …

'Got it!' El shouted triumphantly. 'You might have told me it was Mum's birthday.' She pushed open the door. 'Quick, before Honey finds us!' she cried, as she charged into the workroom. Meg followed, leaving Callie to close the door and snap on the fluorescent lighting strips. The room brightened. El looked around in satisfaction.

'Okay Meg, show us what you've got,' she demanded.

Meg bent to her schoolbag and scratched around. 'Damn,' she said, 'I can't find my organiser. I must have left it on the bus this morning.'

'Don't tell me you've lost the photos you took?'

'No.' Carefully, she extracted a small bundle of photographs from her biology textbook and fanned them out on the workbench. El bent to study them.

'You haven't got one of Greg!' she protested.

'That's cos he's not coming.'

'Then neither is he.' El thrust the photograph of the new guy and his dreadlocks into the pocket of her school uniform.

Curiosity had got the better of Callie. In spite of her annoyance, she was also giving Meg's collection a careful study. Now she picked up the photo of Lev and waved it under Meg's nose. 'Why have you got him?'

'I dunno.' Meg shrugged. 'We said off-the-wall, and he's so off he's practically a biology specimen.'

'You're right.' El giggled. 'He looks like he's host to

45

all sorts of creatures.' She studied Lev's stained clothes and moth-eaten beanie with a shudder of distaste.

'He's a loser.' Meg cast a mischievous glance at Callie. 'Going nowhere. A bit like the Lady of Shalott, really.'

'So put him in. Then they can sail down the river together,' El instructed.

'I thought she wasn't supposed to die,' Meg objected.

'The Lady loved Lancelot, the perfect knight, not a ...' Callie was going to say 'loser', but her tongue refused to form the words although her brain told her they were probably true. But she'd read something else in Lev's face; something that touched her heart. 'Anyway, Lev can't help the way he looks. He's got nowhere to live and no-one to look after him.'

'How come you're such an expert all of a sudden?'

'I talked to him at school today. I felt sorry for him.'

'Actually, I saw him at recess.' Meg sounded concerned now. 'He was ratting through the rubbish bins. Do you think he was looking for something to eat?'

There was a moment's silence. 'I'll put him in,' said Callie. As she scanned in the photograph, she studied the haunted, desperate expression of their some-time classmate. She was tempted to turn his mouth up in a smile, but knew it wouldn't suit him. 'Maybe the Lady can help him find a better way to live?' she suggested hopefully.

'You're right, Callie! Going there would save him!'

Meg was suddenly full of evangelical zeal. 'But we'll give him a helping hand. We'll give him some music to listen to.' She seized the mouse and drew a round shape in Lev's hand. 'A discman,' she explained.

'Where does he get the money to buy CDs?' El asked.

Meg shrugged. 'If he doesn't want it, he can always sell it.'

'He could use the money for food and shelter,' said Callie.

'It won't get him very far though, will it?'

'Shouldn't he be wearing britches or something?' El reached for Callie's book and flipped through it, looking for an illustration.

'You could give him a suit of armour, like Lancelot,' Meg suggested.

Callie shook her head as the image of her perfect knight flashed through her mind: armour gleaming silver in the sun as he straddled the white stallion, shield raised and lance at the ready. 'No,' she said sharply. 'You have to earn a knighthood.'

'He looks silly in those dirty jeans,' Meg interjected as she studied the dishevelled figure on the screen. 'Actually, he looks kind of lost.'

Callie glanced in her direction, surprised that Meg too, had been touched by the desperation in Lev's face.

'Here!' El stabbed a finger at a picture, thrusting the book under Callie's nose for inspection.

'Okay.' The figure on the screen shed its twenty-first

century grunge, donning instead breeches, stockings and shoes, topped by a woollen tunic.

'Okay, who else?' El turned from the four figures on the screen to the photos on the workbench. 'We need another two guys to even things up. What about him?' She picked up the photo of the guy on the bus.

'Stephen,' Meg said thoughtfully. 'That's what they called him. Did you notice? Not Steve or Stevo. Stephen.'

'Yeah. And they didn't want to sit with him either.' There was a malicious gleam in El's eyes.

'But he seemed to have plenty of mates. He spent his whole time on the phone.' Callie scanned the photograph as she spoke, watching Stephen's features appear on screen.

'But did you listen to what he was saying? Bribing the first one with the fact that he'd got some notes or something for him. And he was boasting about his night out to the second one.'

'He told the guy he should've come. I bet he asked him and the guy said no, so then he had to rub it in that he'd had a great night without him.' El peered over Callie's shoulder, giving Stephen's image a disapproving frown.

'So shall I take him out, then?'

'Leave him. But you'll have to change the uniform. Dress him like the other guy, but more classy.' El grinned at Meg. 'You can have him,' she said. 'He's obviously got heaps of dough. He's a good catch.'

'Gee, thanks.' Meg looked sour.

'He's not bad-looking,' Callie commented, as she changed his clothes. 'Pity he's so up himself.'

'You've forgotten something.' Meg's frown of resentment changed to a smile as she took the mouse from Callie and sketched a mobile phone in Stephen's hand.

'So he's got a phone, and Lev's got a discman. What about us?' asked El.

'That's easy.' Callie took the mouse from Meg and keyed in a graphic of a guitar, which she rested against a stone wall in the tower. Head tipped to one side, she inspected it, then deftly altered the shape, capturing the round belly of a lute. 'That's more like it,' she said.

'If I've got my music, you'd better take your paintbox,' Meg suggested.

Callie slotted a bulky box under the green-robed figure's arm. 'What would you like to take?' She turned to her sister.

'Oh … um …' El looked startled. She wasn't often caught out. 'Pass,' she said.

'You don't get off that easily,' Meg joked, making the most of the unexpected opportunity to keep El off-balance.

'I can't tuck a swimming pool under my arm!' El defended herself, flexing her shoulders and doing a couple of butterfly strokes in the air. 'Or a tennis court.' She added a few practice swings to her actions.

'A tennis racquet?' Callie raised the mouse.

'That's not much use,' Meg objected. 'I thought you wanted to be a doctor. Why don't you take a stethoscope or something?'

'That's Dad's crazy idea, not mine,' El grumbled. 'He's got this notion that Callie should go into business, even though she spends all her time drawing and painting, and I'm supposed to do medicine cos I used to like dressing up in a nurse's uniform when I was little. It's really stupid.'

'But it was your idea to do that course in first aid. And you said you enjoyed it. You went really well too,' Callie pointed out.

'Yeah, but then I fainted when Leah had that nosebleed in class. I hate the sight of blood!'

'You'd get used to it if you were a nurse,' said Meg. 'You always told me you wanted to work in a hospital when you grew up.'

'Yeah, well Dad's made up his mind I'll be a doctor or nothing. And seeing I'll never get the marks to do medicine, I guess I'll be a nothing.'

'Rubbish!' said Callie. 'You just need to convince Dad that nursing is what you want to do with your life, that's all.'

'Like you've convinced him you want to be an artist, you mean?' El retorted.

Callie reddened and turned away to study the screen. 'Make up your mind. What do you want to take with you?'

'I'll think about it while you scan Greg.' El rummaged through her pockets and pulled out a crumpled, much-thumbed photograph of her boyfriend. 'Gotcha!' she chortled as she thrust it into Callie's hands. 'I thought I'd better bring one, just in case.'

'That's not fair,' Meg complained. 'I wasn't allowed to have who I wanted, so why should you?'

'Cos I don't want anyone else,' said El, glancing at her watch. 'Come on, we're wasting time.' She pushed Meg out of the way so she could stand over Callie. 'Greg and I have been going out for yonks, so I want him in the tower with me.'

'He'd go barking mad with boredom.' Callie stood up and faced her sister. 'No footy way back then. No swimming or surfing either.'

'Just put him in.'

'This is silly.' Callie made no move to obey El. 'I don't want to do this.'

'Then I'll do it.' El grabbed the photo from Callie.

'No!' As Meg lunged towards El, she crashed into Callie, sending her reeling against the motion platform.

'Watch out!' But El's shout came too late.

Callie's hand hit the control panel. Desperately, she scrabbled at levers and knobs, trying to break her fall. The screen shrieked, then went blank. The world blacked out. Callie could see nothing, hear nothing. But she could feel herself falling, spinning through an icy, rushing darkness that enveloped and swallowed her. There was nothing to hold on to. Nothing above her, nothing below. Yet she sensed El's and Meg's presence, and took comfort from the fact that she was not alone. And still she kept falling. Falling through time. Falling through giddy, echoing space, falling through emptiness. Falling.

CHAPTER FOUR

Icy darkness melted into grey warmth. Callie stretched out a foot and took a tentative step. Something bulky was wedged under her arm; she shifted its weight to the other side. She held out her free hand to stop herself from bumping into anything, and took another step.

Something solid barred her way. She pushed, but it was too heavy to move. Her fingers explored a flat surface, wood rough and splintery. A table? She frowned. There was nothing like that in her father's laminated plastic and steel workroom. She dropped the large box under her arm onto the wooden surface and screwed up her eyes, trying to see through the haze.

Had her father's computer blown up? Had she gone blind?

Panicking now, she stretched out both arms and took a step in another direction. Her foot landed on something soft.

'Ow!' An outraged howl followed immediately on the contact. 'Get off!'

'Who's that?'

No answer, just a hoarse squeak. But Callie had recognised the voice.

'El? It's me!'

'Callie?' El's voice cracked as she cried out. 'Where are you? I've gone blind. I can't see!'

'Neither can I,' Callie comforted her.

'I can't see either.' Meg's voice came from some distance away, followed by the gruffer tones of a male voice. 'What the …? Bloody hell, where am I? What's going on?'

The voice sounded vaguely familiar. Callie squinted, trying to see.

The haze was lifting; ghostly shapes gradually took on colour and clarity, revealing grey stone walls and rough-hewn furniture. Terrified and amazed, Callie looked around her.

The scene was familiar: the stone walls of the tower, the ladies in their long dresses, the men in tunics and breeches. Callie pinched the soft flesh under her forearm. Hard. It hurt. She was one of the ladies, then. So were Meg and El. Real. Breathing. Just like the two guys with them, Lev the lost, and Stephen, the loud-mouth show-off on the bus.

Callie closed her eyes and wished as hard as she could that by the time she'd counted to ten, she would find that it had been an hallucination and that everything was back to normal.

She counted slowly aloud, then opened her eyes. They were all still there, unmoving, just as she had scanned them onto the screen. Were they real? Or had she imagined their voices?

Then Meg spoke again. 'Where are we?' Puzzled, she smoothed the skirt of her blue silk gown. 'Why are we dressed like this? What's happened to us?'

'I don't know.' Callie was torn between panic and a growing exhilaration. She could hardly believe what she was thinking.

'Well, we'd better find out.' El clutched up her long skirt and rushed across to the shuttered window. She flung the shutters open and peered outside, expecting to see the familiar surroundings of her father's workroom. She cast one appalled glance at the scene then reeled back, to face Callie with an accusing stare. 'Okay, you've had your fun. Now take us back!' She took a step forward and tripped on the hem of her gown. Staggering, she clutched at the nearest object, trying to regain her balance.

Stephen shook her hand off, an expression of anger twisting his face. 'I remember you. You were on the bus this morning.' He checked them out in turn. 'What's going on? What are we doing here? Why are we dressed up like this?'

He fired his questions at Callie. She realised that somehow, even Stephen knew that this was her fault. 'I don't know,' she confessed. 'I just don't know.'

'But you can do something about it, right?'

'What can I do?' Callie shrugged. 'I guess something happened when I fell against the control panel of the VR machine. I must have triggered something to bring us onto the screen.'

'We're not on a screen!' El flapped a hand towards the window. 'Take a look outside. I think we're really there.'

'There?' Callie rushed to the window. 'You mean we're in Camelot?'

'Yes. I don't know what you were playing at on Dad's computer, but you seem to have zapped us back to medieval England.'

'Let me think!' Callie felt dazed, overcome by the questions shouting in her mind. How had she managed to access the graphics on the computer? How had she managed to put them into the story? Fascinated, she stared out across golden fields of ripening crops; at green meadows starred with yellow and white daisies; at the tangled forest and the gleaming river threading towards a walled medieval city. 'I don't believe it!' she whispered.

She staggered and almost fell as she was roughly shouldered aside by Stephen. His body blocked the window as he leaned out, peering down at the scene below.

'There's no such place as Camelot, so how can we be there?' He swung around to confront her. 'You can't send us somewhere that doesn't exist.'

'It looks pretty real to me,' El grumbled, stepping forward to stand beside Callie.

'Maybe we're not here?' Callie ventured. 'Maybe we just think we're here?'

'Of course we're here,' El contradicted. 'You only have to look out of the window to prove that.'

'Maybe time isn't linear, maybe it's more like a loop?' Meg drifted over to the window to check the scene.

'What's that supposed to mean?' Stephen demanded.

'That all of time, past, present and future, exists at once. And somehow we've managed to move from now to then, we've jumped the loop through Callie's program?' Meg paused for a moment to consider. 'Or maybe we've slipped down one of those wormhole things?'

'And travelled through time?' Stephen shook his head. 'You have to be joking. But I'm not laughing. Wherever we are and whatever you've done, we have to get out of here. Now!'

'Maybe time's forked?' Meg said dreamily, ignoring him. 'Maybe we've slipped into a parallel universe where Arthur really existed.'

'Are you suggesting we've left the program, that we're back in the real time of Arthur Pendragon, the one who actually existed some time in the sixth century?' Callie jigged up and down in excitement. 'I've read about him. After the Romans abandoned Britain, Arthur was the Dux Bellorum who united the Celts against the barbarian Saxon invaders. There was peace in Britain for ages afterwards, at least until Mordred and Arthur managed to kill each other at the Battle of Camlann.'

'Look, this isn't a game, or a history lesson. I have to get home. So what are you going to do about it?' Stephen demanded.

Callie blushed, and shook her head.

'I think it's a fantastic achievement to bring us here, even if we're not quite sure where we are or how we're going to get back.' Meg frowned at Stephen, then turned back to the window. 'If this is real, I think we should make the most of it. Let's go out and explore.'

'Are you mad!' El stamped her foot. 'Gran will call the cops if we don't come home. And what about Greg? I promised I'd ring him after tea. You have to think of something, Callie!'

'Perhaps we've come here for a reason?' Meg questioned. 'Maybe we're supposed to stop the battle at Camlann, change the future of Camelot in some way?'

Callie's stomach took a nosedive as she heard Meg put her fantasy into words.

'Change the course of history?' El interposed.

'Or maybe just change the story.' Meg smiled at Callie.

Stephen strode across the room and grasped Callie's arm. 'We're wasting time on this fantasy rubbish. You've got to take us back. I have to go home.'

'Tell me how, and I will.' Callie prised his fingers off and faced him, daring him to touch her again.

Stephen's mouth tightened in anger. 'I can't stay here. I've got more important things to do with my time than take part in your silly experiments.'

'I'm sorry, but I really don't know how to access our own time. I need my dad's computer. And there's nothing like that here.' Callie gestured at the room and its contents: a four-poster bed with canopy and drapes, a rough table and several benches, a squat wooden cupboard with a jug and basin set on top, beside a mirror with an elaborately carved wooden frame.

The mirror? Was it significant somehow? It seemed the answer was there, if only she could grasp hold of it. But the fleeting glimpse of an idea faded, along with her brief spurt of hope, and she was left confronting reality — if that was what it was.

A stunned silence followed Callie's announcement.

'I can't afford to waste time mucking about here,' Stephen said urgently. 'I'm doing the HSC this year. My parents will spew if I go missing.'

'This is unreal,' Lev interrupted unexpectedly, a dreamy smile on his face as he checked out his surroundings. He was the only one who hadn't yet moved or asked any questions. 'I've never been any place like this before.' He put down the discman, then snatched it up again as he realised what he'd been carrying. 'Cool!' he said, and switched it on. 'I've always wanted one of these.' He put the earphones on and listened intently. 'It's not working,' he said then, checking that there was a CD in place. 'I guess it needs new batteries.' He put the discman down again and looked about him. 'Where are we anyway?'

'Camelot.'

'That's crazy!' A sudden fit of coughing shook his thin frame.

'Tell me about it.' Stephen turned on Callie. 'This is all your fault,' he accused.

'I was the one who pushed Callie. If it's anyone's fault, it's mine.' Meg turned away from the window and propped herself against the table. 'Isn't it weird,' she said. 'This place is just like it was when we walked around in Callie's program, except there are lots of other things too, like those tapestries on the walls, and those woven rugs on the floor … and a really funny smell.' She looked down, her nose wrinkling as she inspected the crumbs of food and dried flowers trapped among the rushes that covered the floor.

'It's called BO.' El cast a venomous glance at Lev.

Meg pushed the shutters at the side of the window, opening them wider. She leaned out and took a deep breath. 'I can also smell cooking,' she said, sniff-testing the air. 'I'm starving. Do you think we can find someone to give us something to eat?'

'What if no-one can see us?' Callie suggested. 'I mean, if we've somehow slipped back or forwards in time ...'

In the silence that followed her words they could hear the distant, monotonous clanging of a church bell. 'It's coming from Camelot,' Meg said. 'Look.' She pointed to the walled city beyond the fields.

The sudden sound of voices and a brief howl of misery floated upwards. Meg leaned further out the window, looking down. 'I can't see anyone,' she said, disappointed.

'The sounds come from nearby, though.' Callie listened intently. 'Inside this building. People must be living here.'

'That's it! I've had enough. I really can't take this time travel stuff seriously.' Stephen patted the pockets of his tunic. With a satisfied smile, he extracted his mobile phone.

'What are you doing?' Callie could hardly believe her eyes as she watched him punching the buttons.

'Phoning home. What do you think?' He lifted the phone to his ear, his expression a mixture of expectation and fear.

'Home hasn't been discovered yet, ET.' El rolled her eyes. 'How do you expect to get through?'

Stephen turned his back, ignoring her. Callie held her breath, half-hoping, half-fearing a replay of one of the morning's conversations on the bus.

Tony! Mate!

But Stephen stayed silent.

'Nothing happening?' Callie asked, when she couldn't stand the suspense any longer.

He shook his head, disconsolate. 'It's not even ringing,' he said, as he folded it away.

'You'd better hide that,' Callie advised. 'If there are people around, we'll have to look as normal as possible. Otherwise they might think we're witches or something. They might try and burn us at the stake.'

'Ugh!' Meg shuddered. 'I hope you're joking.'

'No.' Callie looked around the room, remembering the artefacts she'd drawn in. There was Meg's lute, propped against the wall. And the box of paints on the table where she'd dropped it earlier. Now she knew what the chunky box under her arm had been. She wished she'd drawn in a computer instead. Except that wouldn't have worked either.

'I'll hide the discman.' She bent over and picked it up.

'No! It's mine!' Lev lunged forward, but El pushed him out of the way. He staggered, then collapsed abruptly onto the floor. 'It's mine,' he whined.

'Look at us! Stuck in the Middle Ages with a deadbeat on our hands,' El grumbled.

'If that's where we are,' said Meg. She pinched her lip thoughtfully between finger and thumb as she watched Callie push aside the drapes of the huge four-poster bed and shove the discman under the long bolster that served as a pillow.

'At least we're dressed right. We should blend in okay.' Meg looked down to check out her outfit. She frowned as she noticed her bare wrist. 'Anyone got the time?' she asked. But no-one was wearing a watch.

'It was just after five when I checked in Dad's workroom.' With a swish of silken skirts, El walked over to the window and peered out. 'The sun's climbing up the sky. I reckon it's still quite early in the morning here.'

'Give me your phone, Stephen.' Callie held out her hand. 'I'll hide it with the discman.'

'But what am I doing here? Can you tell me that?' Stephen sounded belligerent, but his face was pale with shock as he handed the phone to Callie. 'I mean, I don't even know you. And I don't want to know you either. So why have you brought me here?'

'For fun,' El said quickly, as Callie tucked the phone underneath the feather bolster.

'Fun? You called me a retard.' He glared at El.

'Fighting each other isn't going to solve anything,' Meg broke in quickly. 'I reckon we should all go out and explore. Maybe there's something outside that can help us get back?'

'I can't leave the tower!' Callie looked suddenly frightened. 'I'm the Lady of Shalott, remember? And my fate is to die.'

'Nonsense!' El grabbed her arm and hugged her close. 'The Lady of Shalott didn't have us on her side. We're going to do things differently. That's why we set it up the way we did.' She considered Callie thoughtfully. 'The first thing you must remember is, no peering at old Lancelot out of the window.'

'The Lady of Shalott? What are you rabbiting on about now?' Stephen looked from El to Callie in angry frustration.

'We'd better introduce ourselves,' Meg tried to pacify him. 'I'm Meg Atkins and the twins are Elaine and Charlotte Leblanc, or El and Callie for short.' As Meg explained what they'd been doing with the virtual reality program, El drew Callie aside.

'We've got to get home,' she whispered urgently. 'Can't you think of something?'

'What? I just don't know what to do.' Callie searched the room for inspiration, while her mind fantasised over being rescued by a handsome knight on a huge white horse …

'Hey!' A sharp elbow in her side jerked her back to their predicament. Her gaze came to rest on the squat brown box on the table. Painting? The mirror?

'The Lady of Shalott stayed in the tower weaving scenes she could see in the mirror,' she said slowly. 'I don't know how to weave, and I haven't got Dad's computer to re-create our home, but what if I try and paint us back?'

'You mean, do a painting of our house?'

'Yeah. The poem says something about the mirror's magic sights. If it's a magic mirror, maybe I can get it to reflect the painting of our house, and then —'

'We'll be magically transported home?' El's voice was thick with sarcasm. 'Get real!'

'Well, you think of something better.'

There was a brief silence. Everyone looked at El for the answer. It was what they usually did. Callie half-hoped her sister would come good. Part of her was terrified, and wanted most desperately to be safe among familiar surroundings. But the other part …

'I can't think of anything,' El acknowledged, sounding resentful. She sighed and collapsed heavily onto a bench. 'I guess you'd better give it a try.'

'But what can I paint on? There's no paper here. And only the monks had access to parchment, for illuminating those old texts from the Bible and stuff like that.'

'Paint on this.' El jumped up and strode over to

the large four-poster bed. 'Ugh! Dead animals.' Nose wrinkled in distaste, she flung off a fur blanket, then pulled at the coarse linen sheet underneath. She bundled it up into her arms and thrust it at Callie. 'Here. And for goodness sake, hurry. I don't want to stay in this godforsaken place any longer than I have to.'

'Godforsaken?' Meg's voice echoed El's. 'I don't think so. Remember what Ms Hope said about the quest for the Holy Grail? They really believed in God at Camelot.' She flashed a small smile at Callie. 'You paint your picture. I'm going to try something else.'

Picking up her long skirt, she walked over to the lute propped against the wall. 'How do you play this thing?' She grasped the instrument by its neck and tucked it into position. Her fingers curled over the unfamiliar configuration of strings. She plucked a few experimental chords, her expression intent as she tried to make sense of the sounds she was making.

'Oh Lord, start a fire
Lift me up, lift me higher ...' she sang softly, concentrating on the ancient instrument, intent on producing the tune she wanted. She looked up then, daring them to laugh at her. But no-one moved. No-one spoke. They all watched intently.

Meg's voice picked up volume. She began to sway in time to the beat:

'Start a fire in my soul
Hear my words and make me whole,
Take me home, take my pain
Let me burn, burn again ...'

'Shhh! Someone will hear us,' El hissed.
Meg lowered her voice for the refrain:

'Burn, burn again,
Let me burn, burn again ...'

It was a chant she knew well; she sang it regularly at the services she attended. She repeated it several times and then put down the lute. She stretched her hands up above her head and started to talk to God.

'Burn, burn again,
'Let me burn, burn again ...'
Lev continued the simple refrain, adding a tuneless accompaniment to Meg's appeal.

El and Stephen glanced at each other. United in embarrassment, they rushed to help Callie drape the sheet over a stand. As Callie laid out her paints and brushes, El looked around for a tap, then clicked her tongue in annoyance as she remembered where she was. She seized the pottery jug standing on the squat cupboard and tipped out some water into the bowl beside it. 'Here.' She slid the bowl in front of her sister.

'Thanks.' With swift flowing strokes of colour, Callie set about painting the familiar surrounds of their home in Sydney.

Meg continued to pray. And El and Stephen watched in silence, their attention now wholly focused on the possibility of somehow crossing time and space, of somehow getting home.

CHAPTER FIVE

xhausted after her long dialogue with God, Meg opened her eyes and looked around the room.

'We're still here,' El said caustically.

'It might take some time, I suppose.' Meg gave her a tranquil smile. She crossed the room to watch Callie adding a honey-coloured mutt to the scene painted on the sheet. The dog sat outside the workroom, her ears pricked and her expression hopeful.

'That's probably just where Honey is right now. Still waiting for us,' El said sadly.

'That's very good.' Meg tipped her head to one side,

assessing the painting. 'You really should become a professional artist when you leave school.'

'Like our mother?' El exchanged glances with Callie. 'Dad won't allow Callie to go to art school.'

'There are other things you can do as an artist,' Callie said, sounding defensive.

'Like what?' Meg asked.

'Well, combining art with technology for instance.'

'Like you've been doing?'

Callie was shocked into silence.

'Is that what this is all about? Proving you can make art pay?' Meg persisted.

'I —' Callie swivelled around as a loud groan was followed by an agonised retching.

'Oh gross!' They watched, dismayed and disgusted as Lev proceeded to spew his guts out, before collapsing in a heap on the floor.

'Filthy pig.' El aimed a kick in his direction, not quite making contact.

'Don't!' said Meg. 'He can't help it.' She looked away from the vomit stains on Lev's tunic and pants, and the puddle on the floor. Her stomach heaved at the thought of cleaning him up.

'I guess this is what happens when you live out of rubbish bins.' Callie looked down at Lev and wondered what, if anything, they should do for him. She turned to her sister. 'I wish I'd drawn in a medical textbook for you, or something useful like that.'

El shrugged. 'He'll get over whatever's bugging him.'

'But there must be something we can do to help.' Meg bent over and touched her wrist against Lev's forehead. 'He's burning up,' she said anxiously.

'I suppose we could try and get him clean.' El grabbed the bowl of paint-stained water Callie had been using. Tearing a bit off the sheet that hadn't been painted on, she dipped it in water and wiped Lev's face and clothes. 'You.' She pointed at Stephen. 'And you.' Her finger sliced sideways in Meg's direction. 'Turn him over onto his side. Check his tongue, make sure he can breathe okay, otherwise he'll choke.'

'Turn him over yourself,' Stephen sniffed.

'You want to clean up the sick on the floor then?' El held out the cloth to him.

Stephen stiffened. His lips curled back in distaste. 'I'm not responsible for any of this. And I'm certainly not taking responsibility for … for that.' He jerked a thumb at Lev's inert body.

'Help me, Callie.' Meg dropped to her knees and gently rolled Lev onto his side. She placed a hand on his chest, feeling for the regular rise and fall of his breath. Looking concerned, she bent and placed an ear over Lev's mouth and listened intently.

They waited in silence, watching her.

Lev took a sudden shuddering breath, and then another. And then he stopped breathing. Anxiously, they waited for some sign of life. But there was nothing.

'Do something!' Meg commanded, her voice shrill with panic.

El dropped the smelly rag into the bowl and grasped Lev's wrist between her fingers. Her eyes flicked automatically to her watch to time his pulse, but her wrist was bare. Her grip tightened, but there were no beats to count. Anxiously she shifted her fingers to a new position and tried again.

'I'd better start mouth-to-mouth.' She looked at Lev with an expression of distaste.

'Be careful you don't catch something. You don't know where he's been or what he's been doing,' Stephen warned.

El glanced up at him. 'You seem to know all about it. You do it.'

'No way.' Stephen brushed his hands together, fastidiously wiping away any responsibility for Lev's life. Or death. 'Just roll him onto his back. Tip back his head and pinch his nostrils with your fingers. Then breathe into his mouth — just a few quick breaths. Then wait.'

'I know what to do.' El flopped down beside Lev and rolled him over.

'Here.' Quickly, Callie ripped off a small corner of the sheet and placed it over Lev's mouth.

El bent and gently puffed air through the sheet into Lev's open mouth, while Meg squatted beside her and rested the flat of her hand on Lev's chest.

'Try it again,' Stephen ordered, when there was no response.

This time they all leaned over, watching for the air to deflate from Lev's lungs.

A ragged cheer broke out as Lev's chest rose and fell. El breathed into him one more time, and then again, just to be sure.

'Well done,' Stephen said. El gave him a disgusted look and felt for Lev's pulse once more. This time her fingers picked up a faint throbbing.

'It's a bit irregular, but it'll do for now.' She rolled him onto his side once more, then stood up, pleasure in her accomplishment giving way to concern as she remembered where they were. 'We should get him home. He needs proper medical attention.'

'For an upset stomach?' Stephen sneered.

'It's more serious than that. Some sort of gastric thing, maybe. If he's been living on the street, who knows what he might have picked up.' El looked at Callie. 'What's happened with the painting?'

'I forgot all about it.' Callie picked up the mirror from the top of the cupboard and angled it carefully so that the scene on the sheet in front of her was reflected in the mirror. 'Perhaps we should all make a wish?' she suggested awkwardly.

'Or pray?' Meg added.

'You already tried that,' El said brusquely.

They waited and watched, not quite sure what to do or what to expect.

'It's not going to work, is it?' Meg finally broke the silence.

'Perhaps it's because you haven't included any of us in the scene?' Stephen suggested.

'Oh!' Callie reached for the paintbox. Her hands shook with tension as she hastily painted in their figures with less than her usual care.

'I look like a red turkey,' El said crossly. 'Anyway, why are you painting us in these stupid old clothes?' She flicked a finger against the rich scarlet silk of her gown. 'Put us in our twenty-first century gear. That's where we want to go.'

Embarrassed and self-conscious, Callie tried to update their clothes. But the paint was still wet. The colours ran, obscuring their features, turning everything into a muddy blur.

Humbled, she put down her brushes and, without looking at the others, held the sheet to the mirror once more.

'Is it working?' Meg had gone to sit beside Lev. Her hand on his chest monitored his breathing, but her anxious gaze was fixed on Callie's face.

'No.'

'What are we going to do?' El reached over and grabbed Callie by the shoulder. 'This is all your fault.' She gave her sister a hard shake. 'You've got to think of something else.'

'And while you do, I suggest we follow Meg's idea and go exploring,' Stephen drawled. 'We'll see if we can find out just where we really are. Meg? You can come with me.' He turned to El. 'And you can stay and look after your friend.'

'If we're going anywhere, we have to stick together,' she retaliated.

'That's impossible. For a start, he's not able to move.' He pointed down at Lev. 'As for you,' he confronted Callie, 'if you think you're the Lady of Shalott, you'd better stay up here and … I don't know. Weave something.'

'I don't know how.'

'Then keep on painting. Try another Australian scene. Maybe this time it'll work?'

'Who do you think you are, giving us orders and telling us what to do?' El demanded.

'Coming here wasn't my idea.' Stephen surveyed her coolly. 'I wasn't responsible for getting us into this mess. But seeing none of you seems to have the slightest idea how we're going to get out of it, I've decided to take charge.'

'What gives you the right?' Hands on hips, El faced him.

'I'm the oldest. And I've got brains. I've been around. I've had more experience than any of you. So I'm making the decisions. Come on, Meg. Let's go.'

'Yessir! Right away, sir.' Meg snapped off a quick salute.

'I want to come too.'

'And risk leaving that deadbeat there?' Stephen turned his back on El. 'I'd rather you came with me than that bossy, loud-mouth friend of yours,' he told Meg.

'How dare you!' El's fists clenched. She stepped forward.

'I don't mind staying,' Meg volunteered, anxious to keep the peace. She knew El couldn't bear to be left out of anything. 'You go exploring with Stevo.' She patted her stomach. 'Maybe you can find us something to eat?' she added hopefully.

'My name is Stephen.' He followed El as she stomped out of the room.

'Good luck!' Callie called, suddenly anxious. 'Come straight back if there's any trouble.'

'Don't you go looking out the window at old Lancelot while we're gone,' El retaliated. The heavy wooden door swung closed behind them.

Meg looked at Callie. 'Now what?'

'You heard what King Stephen ordered. I guess I'd better get to work.' Callie draped the sheet, angling it so that she had a square of clean linen in front of her. She sloshed the stinking vomity water out of the window, rinsed the bowl, then poured some clean water into it. Standing with her back to the window, she pulled her paintbox towards her.

'Are you going to paint what you see, or paint something from home?' Meg asked.

Callie shrugged. 'Last time I painted home, it didn't work,' she said. 'Maybe I ought to paint what I can see in the mirror?'

'Just like the Lady of Shalott?' Meg sounded anxious. 'You don't want to be like her. Remember what happened?'

'I don't expect Sir Lancelot to come riding by.' Callie tried to laugh, but the sound caught in her throat. Now that she was stuck with the role of the lady in the tower, she realised that she was frightened. With an awful sense of foreboding, she picked up the brush and looked into the mirror.

And drew in her breath with a sudden gasp of shock, of amazed recognition.

The flower-speckled meadows were there, and so was the river snaking glitter bright through the dark green trees. But Callie's attention was focused on the sun-dappled highway, and on the distant figure of the knight riding in her direction.

'Oh!' Her fingers tightened around the brush. She reached for the paintbox, suddenly desperate to capture forever the image coming steadily towards her. As she sketched frantically, the knight's features became clearer. But she knew them already. They were etched into her mind and into her heart, just waiting to become reality. Her hand flashed across the linen sheet, but she was hardly aware of the painted surface coming to life. Her attention was solely on the mirrored image of her love, her one true knight. Her destiny.

A shaft of sunlight turned the knight's polished helmet into a crown of bright fire. His hair flowed black beneath it, rising and falling with the motion of his body. He sat lightly astride the white stallion. His armour sparkled with the fire of diamonds, and on his black shield a red-cross knight kneeled to a silver queen, just as Tennyson had described him:

> *'All in the blue unclouded weather*
> *Thick-jewell'd shone the saddle-leather,*
> *The helmet and the helmet feather*
> *Burn'd like one burning flame together,*
>   *As he rode down to Camelot.'*

Callie's lips formed the words, and she trembled with excitement and joy. Lancelot was so close! She had only to run to the window and wave to him, and he would come to her!

She whirled around to signal to him, but a question stopped her flight: What would happen then? Crushed, she looked to Meg for the answer.

Meg was leaning over Lev, her ear pressed to his mouth, listening. Callie frowned, anxiety over Lev momentarily pushing Lancelot from her thoughts. But

Meg didn't move; she wasn't trying to resuscitate Lev or anything. He must be okay.

Callie's gaze slid back to the mirror, to the horseman now almost underneath the tower. If she rushed to the window, she was condemned to die. If she stayed by the mirror, he would pass by and she would never know him. She would never find out what she might have achieved. She would never find out why she'd travelled space and time to be here. How could she bear it? She might as well be dead!

As she studied the reflected figure, Lancelot looked up. His dark eyes locked onto hers. His hands tightened on the reins. The horse checked. Lancelot half-rose in his saddle, tilting his head and hunching his shoulders in an awkward bow. He glanced up again, and Callie beckoned to him in the mirror. He raised a hand in greeting then, a friendly salute. But just as she opened her mouth to call out to him, he dug his spurs into the horse's side and galloped on down the highway.

Callie drew a shaky breath. She stretched out her hand to a nearby stool and collapsed onto it, pressing her face down between her knees, almost suffocating in the heavy silken folds of her dress. She pushed her skirt aside, then bent over once more, sucking up air in great greedy gulps. Her heart felt like a pinball ricocheting around her chest. She wondered if she was going to die right now.

'Callie? Are you all right?' A hand shook her gently. Callie came back from a dizzy abyss to find Meg squatting beside her.

'I ... uh ...' She couldn't talk.

'What's happened? Take your time. You look like you've seen a ghost,' she joked, trying to cheer herself as well as Callie.

Callie moistened her lips with the tip of her tongue. 'Lancelot,' she whispered. She pressed a hand over her mouth, regretting her admission. She didn't want to share Lancelot with anyone.

'Lancelot?' Meg's eyes widened as she glanced at Callie's impromptu canvas. 'You actually *saw* him?'

Callie nodded, determined not to say any more. Meg wouldn't laugh at her, she knew that much. But she'd tell El, and El would never let her hear the end of it.

'Oh no! You realise what this means? Once the Lady of Shalott goes to the window —'

'I didn't,' Callie interrupted. 'I painted him from the mirror.'

'Thank goodness.' Meg let out her breath in a gusty sigh. 'There's no harm done, then. He doesn't even know you're here.'

'Yes he does,' Callie admitted. 'I saw him in the mirror. And he saw me. He bowed and then he waved.' Had she imagined the admiration she'd seen in his eyes? The indecision that had held him just for a moment, until duty prevailed and he'd gone off to join the knights at Camelot. And Arthur. And Guinevere.

A splinter of hatred shredded her heart. She clenched her hands together, feeling her nails dig into her palms. The pain helped to calm her.

'If he saw you, that means El and Stephen can be seen too.' Meg sounded worried. 'I hope they're managing all right.'

'They're not mentioned in the ballad,' Callie said slowly. 'Maybe they won't be seen? Maybe only the Lady of Shalott is visible?'

'Maybe.' Meg looked at her with frightened eyes. 'What's going to happen to us?' she wailed.

'We all know what happened to the Lady.' Callie tried to come to terms with what it meant. 'Maybe I'll have to relive the myth? Relive it … and die!'

'And maybe the rest of us will be stuck here forever. Like invisible nothings. As if we'd never been born!' Meg gripped hold of Callie's hands. 'Please take us home,' she whispered. 'I hate it here. I don't want to stay!'

'I'll try.' Callie comforted her. 'We'll talk about it when the others come back. Maybe we can work something out.'

She didn't dare tell Meg that she'd changed her mind. She was afraid, yes, but underneath the fear her heart thrummed with a steady, pulsing joy. She had seen Lancelot. She might see him again. It was worth staying, just for that.

CHAPTER SIX

'ook what we've found!' El sang out, kicking at the door until Meg opened it. She beamed complacently at her friend over her laden arms.

'Food! Fantastic!' Meg grabbed a silver platter of sliced meat and several small chickens from El, her expression changing from ecstatic to dubious as she asked, 'Any salad?'

'No, nothing like that.'

'I found some fruit.' Stephen set down the jug he was carrying then pushed a platter in front of Meg. 'Plums. And pears and apples.' He carefully selected the ripest of the plums and presented it to her.

She took it with a smile of thanks. 'Maybe I should wash it first?' She paused in the act of popping it into her mouth.

'The water's probably dirtier than the fruit. They weren't too hot on hygiene in those days.'

Meg inspected the plum then shoved it into her mouth. 'Mmmmm.' She closed her eyes, savouring the sweet juice.

'And I found some cheese. And bread.' El laid another dish on the table.

'Knives and forks? Plates?' Callie's stomach gave a hungry gurgle.

'We couldn't find anything like that.'

'Couldn't you ask nicely?'

Stephen hesitated. 'There were people coming and going. Servants carrying these platters of food. But they ignored us. They didn't say anything when we helped ourselves to this stuff. So it's —'

'That's because they couldn't see us. I already told you that,' El interrupted.

Stephen shrugged. 'So it's help yourself with fingers time.' He tore off a drumstick and gnawed at the flesh with sharp, white teeth. 'This chicken tastes like rubber hosepipe,' he said.

'That's cos it's probably a pigeon.'

Stephen pulled a face, but he kept on chewing.

'So you reckon nobody saw you?' Meg checked.

'No.' El got in before Stephen had a chance to answer.

'Well, Lancelot saw Callie all right. He waved to her.' Meg licked her juice-stained lips and wiped her sticky fingers down her skirt.

'Callie!' El looked at her sister. 'You went to the window?'

'No, I didn't.' Callie was sorry Meg had raised the subject of Lancelot, even though the evidence was in front of them all. 'I watched him in the mirror, and I painted him. That's all.'

El hurried over to inspect Callie's work. 'He looks just like when you drew him before,' she observed. She wouldn't admit to Callie what she was actually thinking: that the guy was really something!

Callie didn't reply. Just the thought of Lancelot choked her up.

'Why are you wasting time painting him when you're supposed to be painting scenes of home to get us back?'

'I couldn't help it.' Trying to deflect her sister's anger, Callie walked over to the food and piled some sliced meat onto a chunk of bread. 'Want some?' she offered, holding it out.

El ignored her. 'You're not to have anything to do with Lancelot. We're not here for that.'

'Oh yes we are.' Callie surprised herself. Until she'd spoken, she'd had no intention of revealing her plans to anyone, least of all El.

'We are not!' El's fingers tightened on the corner of the painted sheet.

'I'm not leaving here until I've met him. Until I've spoken to him.' The plan unfolded in Callie's mind as she said the words aloud.

'Don't be such a fool!'

'I'm not wasting this chance. Don't you see? I can't leave until I've tried to do what I came here for.'

'And what's that?' El's tone was icily polite.

'I want to meet Lancelot. I want to try to make him fall in love with me. I want to change the legend so … so King Arthur and his knights conquer Mordred and his armies, and they all stay united to carry on the kingdom of Camelot. I'm not painting any more pictures of home until I do that.'

'Callie!' Meg stifled a giggle.

El tugged the sheet from the stand and ripped off the portrait of Lancelot. 'Your job is to paint us home,' she gritted. She crumpled up the portrait and stepped to the window.

'That's mine! Give it to me!' Callie shrieked. She lunged forward, but El fended her off with a hard shove.

'There. It's gone,' she said, as she threw Lancelot's likeness out of the window.

El's push sent Callie reeling backwards. She tripped and fell, her outflung arm connecting with the mirror as she tried to save herself. It toppled over and smashed into glittering fragments on the hard, stone-flagged floor. Callie stared at the broken mirror, her face ashen.

'Out flew the web and floated wide; The mirror cracked from side to side ...'
Unable to continue, she moistened her lips with her tongue.

'"The curse is come upon me,"' cried the Lady of Shalott.'
Meg finished softly. 'Oh El, what have you done?'
'I ... but I didn't mean ...' El tried to defend herself. 'I don't want Callie to get hurt,' she blustered.

'None of this role-playing will make any difference to what happens to us. I think it's up to us to help ourselves,' Stephen said, as he poured wine into a couple of goblets. 'I suggest we finish this food and then go exploring to see just exactly where we are. Maybe then we'll find some way to get out of this program and go home.' He held out a goblet to Meg. 'We'll have to share, I'm afraid.'

'What is it?' Meg sniffed the liquid.

'Some sort of wine. It was a choice of wine or ale. We thought wine was safer.'

'What about water?' Meg turned to the pottery jug on the squat wooden wardrobe.

'No purification, remember?' Stephen cast a quick glance out the window. 'It probably comes straight from the river where they do their washing, and ...'

'I don't want to know.' Meg picked up the goblet and took a small sip. 'It's quite sweet. It tastes of honey.' She swallowed several mouthfuls, then bent over and offered the goblet to Lev. He opened his eyes and looked at her. Shakily, he reached for the cup and greedily drained its contents. With a sigh, he rolled over and closed his eyes.

Meg reached for a slice of bread and laid a hunk of cheese on it. She crammed it into her mouth and chewed hungrily. Hunger had stilled argument. With the exception of Lev, they were all eating now.

'Should we give Lev something to eat?' Meg asked at last, licking crumbs from her fingers.

'No,' El said quickly, remembering the explosion of vomit. 'He'll only sick it up again. Don't you think?' She appealed to Stephen for confirmation.

'We have to do something about him. He's stinking the place out,' Stephen mumbled through a mouthful of bread and meat.

'Did you find a bathroom on your travels? Maybe we can dunk him in a bath?' Meg asked.

Stephen chuckled. 'There's a long drop down the passage. That's all I could find.' Seeing Meg's puzzled expression, he explained further. 'You know. A chute with a seat over it. Everything goes straight down into the river. That's why you shouldn't drink the water.'

'Yuk!' Meg shuddered.

'He smells disgusting. We have to do something,' said El. Her face brightened as she saw a way to make up for the ground she'd lost. 'I know. Let's take Lev down to the river for a proper wash. The cool water might help bring his temperature down.'

'We'll have to go upstream.' Meg was still recovering from Stephen's revelation. 'I'm not going to risk getting some foul disease from swimming in a polluted river.'

'I'd love to have a swim.' Callie bent her head and tried surreptitiously to sniff her armpits.

'Not you. You've got to stay here and paint us back,' El said firmly.

Callie realised she was being punished. For El's loss of face? Or for bringing them here in the first place? 'You said yourself we should stick together,' she pointed out.

'I told you, no-one can see us. But apparently they can see you. So it's not safe for you to come with us.'

'But —' Callie wanted to say that nothing was safe any more, and that she wanted to be seen — especially by Lancelot. But she was interrupted by Meg.

'Maybe you should stay this time, just while we suss things out?' She sounded slightly apologetic. She didn't want to upset Callie but, like El, she was desperate to get home. 'Try one more painting,' she pleaded. 'Please … while we're gone?'

'No.' Callie folded her arms. 'I'm not painting any more pictures of home.'

'Do it, Callie. You must,' El insisted.

'And what if I did, and I went home without you?' The thought was enough to silence El.

'Anyway, I can't stay and paint cos I haven't got a mirror any more.'

'I don't see why you can't look out the window,' said Meg. 'I mean, you did before, when we first got here, and nothing happened.'

'If we're going to give Lev a bath, it'd be safer if you didn't come,' said Stephen.

Callie wondered sourly how he and El had managed to form such an unlikely alliance. Her mouth tightened in rebellion. 'Then I'll come with you next time,' she said. 'I'm not doing anything to get us home until I've seen Lancelot.'

'You don't know how to get us home at all.'

'I have some ideas.' Callie looked directly into El's eyes, daring her sister to call her a liar.

El grunted. She'd thought she knew her twin, knew how to manage her. She wasn't used to this new, defiant Callie.

'You can come next time,' Stephen promised. 'When it doesn't matter if anyone sees you.' He bent over Lev and shook him. Lev groaned and rolled over. He opened his eyes then, and pushed himself up onto an elbow, looking at Stephen with a puzzled frown.

'Just stay here and paint something. We won't be long.' El wiped her greasy fingers on the sheet then leaned over and helped Stephen yank Lev to his feet. Taking an arm on either side, they frogmarched him out the door.

'See you later.' Meg hesitated, wanting to apologise, wanting to reassure Callie that they really did want her company.

'I guess you just don't want me along.' Callie pre-empted her.

'Of course we do,' Meg reassured her. 'It's just that if people see you and not us, they might take you away somewhere; we might get separated. It's too much of a risk.' Before Callie could argue, she closed the door gently behind her and followed the others down the stairs.

Callie stared resentfully at the closed door. It was going to be a long and lonely afternoon. But at least with them gone she could take care of a problem that had become rather urgent.

After waiting a couple of minutes, she opened the door and peered out. No-one around. It was safe to go exploring. Stephen had talked of a long drop somewhere nearby. She tried the door opposite. A room almost identical to their own. Callie noted the furnishings, and the lack of any personal possessions. Unoccupied then. It would do for the guys. She wondered if it was safe to look out the window in this room. But she didn't dare. If dying was her fate, she wasn't going to risk invoking the curse quite so soon. Somehow she had to get to Lancelot first.

A mirror, similar to the one she'd just broken, caught her glance. She picked it up and tucked it under her arm, just in case. Closing the door behind her, she went on with her exploration, not sure what she was looking for, but expecting the smell to tell her when she'd found it.

But in fact it didn't smell. And it wasn't even a room; more of a cupboard tucked at the far end of the corridor with a wooden bench set against the back wall. Holding her breath just in case, Callie peered down the hole in the middle of the bench. But there was nothing to see: only darkness, and the gentle murmur of the river far below. Carefully, she laid the mirror on the bench beside her, then lifted her gown. She found she was wearing a cotton shift beneath; no undies at all. She wondered how the others were getting on, trying to imagine their journey across the fields to the river, and what might happen when they got there.

'Are you sure we can't be seen?' Meg asked anxiously as they left the tower and headed along a narrow winding road that led towards Camelot and ran in the direction of the river. Lev leaned heavily on Stephen's arm, shuffling and dragging his feet.

'He's not paying any attention to us.' Stephen pointed at a figure coming their way. A farmer, dressed in peasant's clothes, trudged slowly along leading a cow on a halter. He passed them without acknowledging their presence, although his glance flicked over them and seemed to linger on the sagging figure of Lev.

'I reckon we should cut off here.' El gestured at a faint track that forked off towards the green curtain of trees and the river beyond. As they turned down it, a couple of knights on horseback came into view, trotting towards Camelot.

'I wonder if one of them's Lancelot?' El said, as she looked back over her shoulder.

'Let's not take any chances of being seen.' Meg grabbed El and hustled her off down the track. 'It's so lush! I can't get over how beautiful the English countryside is.' She gazed appreciatively at the pale pink dogroses twining their way through the hedgerows, and the myriad wildflowers spangling the grass. Fat bumblebees nuzzled in their bright depths, harvesting pollen, and two gaudy red and black butterflies chased each other over a patch of yellow buttercups.

Meg bent and picked one, and held it under El's chin. 'It really works!' she cried, as El's skin tinted bright gold. 'It means you like butter,' she told her as they hurried to catch up with the others who had disappeared into the forest ahead.

The air grew cool as the trees crowded in, their branches black ribs in the high green vault over their heads. Did this forest still exist? Meg wondered. Or were these trees cut down for furniture and firewood centuries ago? She shivered as she pushed her way along the trail. This was a forest from the dawn of time, the sort of forest where wicked stepmothers abandoned small children and wolves ate grandmothers.

Meg plunged on through the green tunnel. Occasional shafts of sunlight pebbled the track with gold patches as it twisted among the creepers and rotting vegetation that covered the forest floor. It was quiet; not even birdsong broke the silence. But then she heard the whispering water and was rewarded by Stephen's shout: 'I can see the river!'

'Let's go a bit higher, just in case,' El suggested as they came out into sunlight and the river spread before them. It looked cool and enticing after their walk. A glittery dragonfly flicked between sunlight and shadows, flirting among the pink and blue flowered spikes growing in profusion along the marshy banks.

'This'll do.' Stephen pushed Lev down onto a grassy patch and stood up, wiping sweat from his face with his sleeve. 'We're far enough upstream. The river should be fairly clean here.' He looked around, then stepped behind a clump of reeds to undress. Showing no such modesty, El undid her girdle with its dangling purse and stripped off her scarlet gown. She giggled as she realised there was nothing underneath her shift. 'Here goes!' she sang, and dived in. She surfaced immediately with a whoop of indrawn breath. 'It's freezing!' she shouted, and set off in a neat but powerful freestyle.

Meg edged behind a bushy screen, stifling a snigger as she caught a glimpse of Stephen's hairy chest and long cotton underpants. He ignored her as he grabbed Lev and flung him, fully clothed, into the river. He jumped in then, and propped Lev up beside him in the shallows. His mouth curling in distaste, he splashed water down Lev's front, rinsing off the worst of the stains.

Feeling embarrassed as her shift swirled out with the current of the river, Meg waded across to Stephen and splashed icy water over Lev's face in an effort to wake him up. The shock of the cold water galvanised him and he yelled and hit out at her.

Stephen caught hold of Lev's arms, pinning them to his side. But Lev struggled and kicked out, yelling at both of them.

'You stupid idiot!' Stephen gritted, unable to stand Lev's behaviour any longer. He shoved Lev down into the water and pushed his head under.

'Don't!' Meg hit out at him, thinking he was trying

to drown Lev. Stephen let him go. Lev came up gasping, spitting out water.

'Let's leave him to soak for a while.' Fed up with playing nursemaid, Stephen set off at a fast pace after El.

Meg watched them go, catching her breath in short gasps as she tried to get used to the icy water. She didn't want to leave Lev in case he got into trouble, although he seemed to have calmed down a bit. He sat, chuckling to himself as he patted the water, sending it skittering in silver drops. But it was freezing just sitting still. So she compromised, swimming carefully around him in a decorous breaststroke, keeping an eye on him as she went.

'I'm frozen. I'm getting out.' Stephen passed Meg on his way back to the river bank. He grabbed Lev and pulled him to the edge. With a relieved shiver, Meg followed. Modesty forgotten in the overwhelming need to get warm, she scrambled up the bank and headed for her dress. Wishing she had something to dry herself on, she bundled the silken gown over her head and hugged the fabric around her icy, goose-bumped body. Stephen too lost no time in dressing, but El, warmed by her vigorous strokes or else just showing off, swam over and grabbed Lev, towing him back into deeper water.

'Wash yourself,' she commanded. 'You're not getting out till you've cleaned yourself up.'

As she shivered on the river bank, and hopped up and down to try and get warm, Meg heard the urgent drumming of a horse's hooves. 'Watch out!' she yelled. 'There's someone coming!'

But it was too late. A shout rang out: 'Stay calm! I'll save you!' And with flying hooves, the white stallion galloped to the edge of the water and skidded to a halt. Silver armour glittered among the sun-dappled shadows as a knight vaulted off the stallion's back.

'Lancelot!' Meg stared at him, recognising him instantly from Callie's painting. But the knight wasted no time acknowledging her. He plunged straight into the river to rescue the drowning couple.

Instantly his heavy armour filled with water and dragged him down. He staggered, then started to flail around. He sank below the surface, then came up again, spouting water in great gasps as he floundered about, searching for a foothold in the soft ooze of the river bed.

Barely able to hide her laughter, El towed Lev back to the shallows, then reached out to grab hold of Lancelot. But Lev clung to her. As he lurched forward, he pushed El onto the river bank then collapsed on top of her and lay inert, breathing heavily from cold and fright.

In a futile effort to regain his dignity, Lancelot stumbled through the muddy shallows, water leaking through the rough links of his chain mail armour. A piece of weed hung from his helmet like a limp green feather. Water seeped down his face, tracking a line of mud. He wiped his eyes and assessed the scene in front of him: a couple standing fully dressed on the river bank; a man dressed but soaking wet, lying sprawled across a half-naked young woman at the edge of the river. There was only one way to read the situation.

'I must congratulate you, sir, on saving this lady's life,' he said gravely as he squelched towards them, hand outstretched to Lev to help him up.

'You what!' El's indignant exclamation was muffled against Lev's body.

'This is a sad welcome to Camelot. From whence have you come? I hope you have not had a long journey?' Lancelot pulled Lev upright, then turned to help El, modestly averting his eyes as Meg ran forward with the scarlet gown.

'Thanks.' Teeth chattering, El took the gown from Meg and pulled it over her head. She hugged herself for warmth and danced a few steps, trying to warm up her chilled feet. She reached for her shoes.

'We're from ... uh ... Australia,' said Stephen.

'It hasn't been discov ...' El spluttered into silence as Stephen tried to give her a warning kick. His foot tangled in the heavy folds of her gown and he hopped about, waving his arms as he tried to keep his balance.

Lancelot frowned at his antics. 'Astra-lay?' he

queried in a deep voice. 'You must mean Astolat? That is not far from here, I think?'

'Far enough.' El's voice trembled with regret.

'I have heard tell 'tis a fine place, though I myself have never been there.' Lancelot drew a scarf from his saddlebag and began to wipe his face clean. Scarf in hand, he bowed to them. 'Allow me to introduce myself. I come from across the water, from Brittany. Sir Lancelot du Lac at your service. Pray tell me your names?'

'El. Elaine.' Flustered by the gaze of the handsome knight, El dropped a curtsey.

'Lady.' He took her hand and pressed it to his lips.

'I didn't think you could see us!' She shivered as his warm lips touched her skin.

'Not see you? But of course I can see you! Do you not remember? I saw you in the tower on my way to Camelot some hours past.'

'That was Callie,' El muttered.

'Callie?'

'Charlotte. Our sister. She has to stay in the tower,' Meg explained, thinking it much safer to let El loose on Lancelot. She shuddered to think what effect he would have on the impressionable Callie. Despite his muddy face and bedraggled appearance, he was devastatingly handsome. A man, not a boy. In fact, he was a lot older than she'd expected.

'How unfortunate for the lady. Is she held in the tower by a spell of enchantment?'

Meg looked at El, then quickly away again. She became aware of her bare feet and hastily tugged her long skirt down to cover them.

'Is your sister a fairy?' Lancelot tried again, when it became apparent no-one would answer his question.

'Fairy?' Stephen spluttered.

'I have heard tell of a marvellous thing.' Lancelot's eyes widened in wonder as he continued. 'News came to Camelot that a magic web floated out of the window of the tower towards some knights riding below. They tell me the web had my likeness upon it! And reapers speak of hearing music, and songs and incantations.' He smiled expectantly, like a small boy hoping to be told a story.

'I'm Meg. Er ... Lady Margaret.' Meg held out her hand, thinking it safest to change the subject. Fast. 'And this is Stephen.' She pointed at him in an attempt to avert disaster. Stephen looked like he was about to explode.

Lancelot kissed Meg's hand and bowed to Stephen. 'And who is our hero?'

'Hero?' Stephen's jaw dropped as he noticed the direction of Lancelot's respectful gaze.

Lev stood dripping, his arms clasped tight around his waist as he shivered with cold and groaned at the pain cramping his belly and limbs.

'I fear you have taken ill from the icy water. Put this around you, sir, before the ague takes you to your death.' Lancelot extracted a long black cloak, glossy as a crow's wing, from a leather bag hanging from the horse's saddle, and folded it around Lev's shoulders. 'Yours was a brave deed, sir,' he said. 'I have known victory in tournaments and in the battlefield, but the river defeated me this day. I could not do what you were able to accomplish.'

'But that's not what —'

Meg nudged El, silencing her protest. 'Lev saved the Lady Elaine's life,' she agreed, 'but Lev is not a sir. He's not a knight.'

'Not?' Lancelot's expression mirrored his disbelief. 'Then you must come with me to the court, sir ... Lev. King Arthur will want to reward you for your heroism this day. I am sure of it.' Used to being in command, he reached up to the horse's jewelled bridle to lead it off, expecting them to follow him.

'What about me?' Stephen reached out to pat the horse's head, trying to ingratiate himself. 'I am not a knight either.' The horse bared its teeth, and he snatched his hand away.

Lancelot's gaze swept over him and dismissed him. 'You will have to earn that honour with some deed of bravery,' he said, soothing the horse with a calming hand. 'But please, will you accompany me to court? King Arthur has been out hunting in the field and so we dine late this day, but I know he will want to welcome you to Camelot. What is your purpose for this visit, may I ask? Do you have business with us?'

'No business,' Stephen said curtly, determined that Lev would receive no honour. 'We are travellers through time and —'

He stopped with an outraged howl as El stepped on his foot, grinding her shoe into his. 'We are most interested to see for ourselves the marvels of Camelot that we have only read about in books,' she said smoothly.

'You are able to read?' Lancelot sounded amazed. 'Only monks and the sons of noble families have that knowledge here in Camelot.'

'There have been great social advances in our part of the world,' El said with a bite in her voice.

Lancelot looked impressed. 'King Arthur will want to hear of all these wonders.' As Lev took a lurching step and almost fell, Lancelot stopped and patted the horse's back. 'I fear your bravery has undone your health. Will you ride into Camelot?'

Lev stared at him with blank eyes. Taking his assent for granted, Lancelot heaved him up and into the saddle. He cast a solicitous glance at El. 'My horse will carry you too, lady, if you wish it?'

'No.' She smiled up at the knight and tucked her arm through his. 'But if you will support me, sir?' She flicked a wink at Meg, who thought of Callie shut away in the tower and felt a stab of pity and anger. El always seemed to get the better of her sister.

'Do you travel alone?' Lancelot called over his shoulder as he led the white stallion with a firm hand, his other arm supporting El.

'Yes.' Meg bent to put on her shoes. 'We have just our brothers for protection.' It seemed safest to pretend they were all one family.

'I'm no brother to that ... that ...' Stephen spluttered, leaning close to Meg so that only she could hear him. 'Do you realise that idiot will become a knight? We'll have to bow to him and show him respect, and call him sir!' He was filled with rage at the injustice of it.

'Never mind.' Meg chuckled. 'I'm sure it'll be very character building for all of us. Especially Lev,' she added, suddenly serious as she thought about the implications. 'I mean, he's never been anything in his life. He's never mattered to anyone. It'll be interesting to see if he lives up to the honour and attention he'll be getting.'

'Fat chance.' Stephen snorted. 'I just hope he doesn't drop us in it. All that talk of fairies and magic! We'll be in great danger if they decide there's something peculiar about us.'

'Then watch your tongue.' Meg looked ahead at the horse and its burden. 'And watch out for Lev too. Dunking him in the river might have cleaned him up a bit, but I think he's still unwell.'

'I bet they'll be sorry they ever made him a

knight!' Stephen's tone left no doubt in Meg's mind that he thought he could live up to the honour of a knighthood, if given the chance.

'If they change their minds about Lev, they might change their minds about us too,' she warned. 'We'll just have to make sure Lev behaves like a knight, okay?' She cast a troubled glance at El, who was turning on the charm, laughing and flirting with Lancelot. He, in turn, seemed to have forgotten the fairy who had so enchanted him that morning; delighted and intrigued, his attention was all on the lady at his side.

'Maybe we should fetch Callie?' Stephen suggested. 'Didn't she want to meet this guy?'

'No. It'll only make things more complicated.' Meg knew who the winner in any contest for a man would be. She glanced sourly at El. 'Callie would go ballistic if she saw them together like this.'

'Do you believe all that stuff about wanting to make Lancelot fall in love with her and changing the legend?'

'El might change it for Callie,' Meg answered obliquely. 'That's if Lancelot falls in love with her instead of with Guinevere.'

'I reckon that would annoy Callie more than anything.' Stephen grinned, then gave a quick shrug. 'But I really can't believe all this stuff.' He pushed aside some thorny brambles and waited for Meg to pass through. 'I mean, I still can't believe we're even here.'

Meg laughed. 'I keep thinking I'm going to wake up

and find myself safely in bed,' she confessed, adding cheerfully, 'But if I do, I'm going to feel really cheated. I must admit I'm curious to know what's going to happen next.'

'Lev's going to be made a knight, that's what.'

'Poor Stephen.' She patted his arm. 'Never mind. Your turn will come. We'll find something heroic for you to do.'

'It's all right for you. You're already a lady!'

'I can thank Callie for that.' And then, as Stephen looked confused, 'When Callie scanned us on the computer, she dressed us as ladies and you two guys as commoners. I'm so glad she didn't make me a milkmaid or a servant or something.'

'But why did she scan me in? Why am I here?'

'We ... uh ... needed company in the tower room. We had a whole lot of photos to scan in but ... well, we didn't have time to add anyone else.' She thought she must sound like a lunatic. And yet the proof was right there. They were living it.

'Then I wish she'd made me more important,' Stephen huffed, seeming to accept Meg's explanation.

'Cheer up. It's who you are inside that counts, not what people call you. Do you feel honourable, Stephen?'

He bit his lip and turned away, quickening his steps to catch up with the others. Was Meg having a go at him? He didn't know.

CHAPTER SEVEN

eg looked about her in fascination as they entered Camelot through the imposing iron gateway. Lean-to hovels cringed against the high walls encircling the town. Grubby children dressed in rags played among piles of smelly rubbish that littered the laneway. Meg held her breath and hurried to catch up with the others, dodging puddles of scummy water along the way.

As they approached the town centre, dirt lanes gave way to narrow cobbled streets lined with timber houses and the larger stone dwellings of wealthy merchants. It was just as Callie had designed it, except now there were people around: noisy children, a woman throwing corn to a few scrawny chickens, an old man pushing a rickety cart.

'What year is it?' Stephen drew closer to Lancelot as they approached the crowded market in the town square.

'Year?' Lancelot reflected. 'The Romans measured time from the birth of Christ in the later years of their occupation of Britain. But we have always followed our own ancient tradition here in Camelot. We honour the wild creatures of the Earth Mother, the Mother Goddess. The present time is known as the year of the wild boar.'

Stephen was momentarily silenced. This was not what he'd expected. He tried again. 'What hour is it?'

Lancelot led his horse to a sundial in the centre of the busy square, and studied it for a moment. The sun slanted across the sky; shadow lay in a dark sliver, marking the hour. Meg wondered how people managed to read the sundial on the wet, sunless days that were more typical of the English climate.

'It is the hour of Vespers,' said Lancelot. None the wiser, Meg stepped up beside Stephen to have a look. As if on cue, a church bell began to toll, a solemn, lonely sound that echoed across the marketplace. Six o'clock. Cages of squawking chickens, bundles of fresh green vegetables and summer fruits lay in haphazard piles on the cobblestones. Traders shouted out their wares: ale, candles, jars of honey, wine and olive oil. The scent of fresh bread set Meg's stomach gurgling in hunger. She felt in the purse dangling from her girdle, wondering if it contained any money. But it was empty.

Maybe she could swap something? She touched the gems around her neck. Bread for a necklace? But her appetite fled at the sight of the next trader, whose stall featured various joints of meat, dark, bloody and fly-infested. She looked quickly away, diverted by the cries of a knife grinder, echoed by the shouts of children thronged around a performing bear. The great beast was dancing to the beat of a small drum played by its trainer. Meg wondered where it had come from, and felt sorry for it.

A couple of mangy cats fought over the half-eaten body of a rat, growling and hissing, defending their prize with sharp teeth and claws. Lancelot kicked out at them as he walked past. They retreated, but kept scrapping over the feast.

The trainer led the bear away on its chain, and the children spilled out across the square, tripping up traders and passers-by as they played a noisy game of tag. Skinny brown dogs, excited by the children's cries, barked and ran in circles, earning curses and kicks from those who stumbled over them.

An old woman, dressed in rags, crossed the street in front of Meg. She was bent almost double under the heavy basket she carried on her back. 'Fa-ggots,' she cried, thrusting a bundle of sticks under Meg's nose. Her voice was hoarse from shouting; her hands filthy and scratched from gathering kindling. As Meg shook her head in regret, Lancelot slipped a coin into the woman's money purse. She bobbed her head and hobbled on.

A man singing a bawdy song and dressed in a fool's costume tapped up to them on roughly carved stilts.

'Boden!' Lancelot shouted a greeting. 'I have not seen you for some months now. Have you been off entertaining your friends across the channel?'

'Indeed I have, Sir Lancelot. But now I am bound for the castle of Camelot. I hope I might have the pleasure of seeing your party tonight?' He gazed down at them all, brown eyes bright with friendly curiosity. He stood quite still on the stilts. Meg wondered how he managed to keep his balance. Lancelot reassured Boden that they would see him soon and they set off once more, stepping carefully. The narrow street was puddled with foul-smelling water and littered with horse droppings and assorted rubbish thrown from the open shopfronts lined on either side. Meg averted her eyes from the ground and studied the displays: goldsmiths and weavers went about their business. The sudden scent of herbs and sweet spices wafted from a man grinding a mixture with pestle and mortar: a sign proclaimed him to be an apothecary. Meg wondered what he hoped to cure with his potions. She walked on past an assortment of leather boots and belts, handmade pottery jugs and dishes, and elaborately carved hair combs made of ivory and wood.

'Wish I could take home some souvenirs,' she said, as Stephen fell into step beside her.

'At least you'd be sure they were genuine and not made in some Asian sweatshop.' He wrinkled up his nose. 'Man, this place stinks!'

'Ssshh!' Meg glanced at Lancelot, wondering if being objectionable was part of Stephen's strategy to prevent Lev from being knighted. But Lancelot was pointing out something to El, giving her the guided tour of Camelot.

Meg stepped aside to make way for a plump, black-garbed priest, who wore a cross to denote his calling. A tall white-robed figure hurried close behind. His hair was shaved in a stripe from ear to ear and he wore no cross, nor any other sign. A trainee priest? He pushed past the black-robed figure and strode on. The priest made the sign of a cross against his retreating back, his face showing nothing of Christian charity.

A druid? Someone who practised the old ways that still controlled the telling of time in Camelot? Was there a battle for power over people's souls going on here?

As they climbed towards the castle, Meg glanced downwards, getting her bearings. The settlement spread before them, bound by thick stone walls.

Beyond was the river, which snaked its course through the fields and past one side of the castle before surging out to the open sea. A barred iron gate in the castle wall gave access to the river and a timber wharf where labourers sweated as they heaved crates and rolled barrels to the waterline. A ship was anchored mid-stream, its tall mast forming a dark cross against the golden evening.

A Christian cross? Lancelot had talked of Christ, but he had also talked of the Earth Mother, the Mother Goddess. Meg wondered if that was why her prayers had failed? Not because she was unworthy, as she'd thought, but because the Mother Goddess held power in this realm?

Then another thought came to her. Perhaps neither Christ nor the Mother Goddess was able to help. Perhaps it was up to the time travellers to help themselves?

'It must have taken a lot of guts to head out to sea in one of those.' Stephen pointed towards the ship that had caught Meg's attention. 'Especially if you believed the earth was flat, and that you might fall off if you got blown off course.'

'Fall off where?' El had dropped back to join them.

Seeing his chance, Stephen stepped forward to catch up with Lancelot and Lev. 'I am older, more experienced and better educated than the one you seek to honour,' he said, as the injustice of the situation fired his bitterness once more.

'Men are knighted for their bravery, not their learning.' Lancelot's tone was coolly indifferent as he propped Lev more securely in the saddle. Lev seemed calm. Either that or he was unconscious.

Suddenly anxious, Meg rushed forward and gave Lev a shake. He looked down at her, grimacing with pain as he stretched out his legs and rubbed his stomach. She hoped he'd stay quiet until they got back to the tower. Her thoughts sped to Callie, wishing they could go back there right now. They'd promised not to be long. Callie would be missing them. She'd be worried.

Reflected in the mirror was the red orb of the sun. Callie watched as it sank slowly through the golden sky. It was very quiet in the tower without the others. But rustles and the odd squeak told her she was not alone. She shuddered, not wanting to think about what was keeping her company.

She studied the painting she'd just finished. Two knights riding past, neither of them Lancelot. Where was he right now? With Guinevere? Callie's fingers clenched tight. Lancelot and Guinevere. It mustn't happen. Not now. Not after everything she'd been through to get here.

She looked into the mirror once more, searching for

him, and saw a knight and a lady walking slowly towards her, arm in arm. As she watched, they stopped and kissed. Frightened, she peered more closely, then relaxed with a breath of relief. The knight wasn't Lancelot. That was all that mattered. She picked up her brush and began to paint in the couple, feeling envious, wishing she too was out in the sweet-scented evening air with its fragrance of roses and honeysuckle, being wooed and courted by Lancelot.

'I'm sick of looking at shadows!' she muttered as she filled the figures with strokes of colour, capturing the red and gold sunset-tinted armour of the knight and the rich hues of the lady's silk gown.

The sun slipped down towards the horizon; in its place rose the moon. Though not full, its light bathed the sky in radiance. The lovers moved slowly out of sight, leaving only the silvery path of the empty highway.

A faint clop-clop of a horse's hooves broke the silence, punctuated by the slow and solemn beat of a drum. A dark shape moved away from the tower. It was a horse, black, with black trappings and plumes, pulling an open cart. The flare from lamps at the back and front illuminated the cart's contents: a large dark box, coffin-shaped, its surface scattered with wildflowers. A small group followed, clinging to each other and wailing their grief.

The knights. The lovers. The funeral. Callie felt

afraid. Everything in the ballad was happening — it was all coming true. And at the end …

I have to meet Lancelot, talk to him, Callie thought. If I'm going to die here, I'll make sure I'm not dying for nothing!

A squeak drew her gaze down to the floor. She stared into the beady eyes of a large brown rat and gave a loud shriek, not caring if anyone heard her.

The rat scrambled up onto the table in a ripple of brown fur and started to scavenge among the remains of their lunch.

'Shoo!' Callie flapped her hands at it, disturbing several other rats that, emboldened by their leader's move towards the food, had also come out to investigate the scene. They paused, then scurried up onto the table to join in the feast.

Callie watched them in the moonlight, shivering with fear and anger. Finally, summoning up courage, she swooped down on the creatures and grabbed the platters from under their furry bodies. In a single movement, she swivelled and hurled the plates of food out of the window.

'There! It's all gone! Now go away!' She flapped her hands at the rats once more. 'Shoo! Shoo!'

They crouched on the table, noses twitching to locate crumbs.

'Go on, get lost!' she hissed as she advanced on them, waving her arms, fighting the hysteria that insisted she run away — out of the room, out of the tower, as far away as possible, preferably back home. 'Go away!' She snatched up Meg's lute and swiped at them, sending them squeaking and scurrying back to their hiding places.

Her skin crawled as she put down the lute and went back to the mirror. She hated rats. And she was angry the others weren't here to help her deal with them. Where were they? Had they vanished into limbo somewhere? She looked into the mirror, searching for signs of them. But the mirror showed only moonlight and emptiness.

Callie sighed and walked over to the bed. She pushed aside the drapes and sank down. The mattress was covered with a soft fur blanket. She stroked it, wondering what fur it was. Rabbit? Cat? Rat?

With a shudder she jumped up and hugged her arms around her body. Now the sun was gone, the air blowing through the open window was cool, too cool for comfort. She longed to crawl into the bed, to hug the warm blanket around her and sleep. But how could she? The rats would come back, would crawl over her and bite her as she slept. She had to keep awake, keep moving. She started to pace the room, to keep warm, to keep the rats away. Where were the others? What had happened to them? Would they ever return?

'I pray you, wait in here.' Lancelot indicated an antechamber off the flower-filled courtyard. He had helped Lev to dismount, then hurried them into the castle. 'I shall inform the king of your presence here, and all that has gone before,' he told them.

Fascinated, Meg checked out their surroundings. No wonder it all seemed so familiar. They had been here before, in Callie's program. It was exactly as she had designed it.

'Arthur Pendragon. Dux Bellorum. High King of Britain.' Lancelot's voice broke into Meg's reverie. 'Sire, may I present our guests?'

Meg sank into a hasty curtsey, trying not to wobble as Lancelot recited their names. She hardly knew how to face the king, this mythical hero whose fame had survived so many centuries. He extended a hand to help her up, several knuckles obscured by the huge dragon seal of the ring on his middle finger.

Beside Lancelot, King Arthur seemed the lesser man despite his elaborate crown and robes. He was shorter, slighter than the knight, and older. But a glimpse of his dark eyes as they appraised the strangers before him convinced Meg that of the two, King Arthur was the wiser and more shrewd. She wondered what he would make of Lev once he had time to get to know him. Her lips twitched as she watched the king listening, with astonished respect, to Lancelot's highly embroidered retelling of how Lev had saved the Lady Elaine from drowning. 'Such bravery,' Lancelot concluded, shaking his head in admiration. 'It was the act of a true hero, a man worthy of knighthood, Sire.'

'No, no, you've got it all wrong!' Stephen couldn't stand it any longer. 'Lev wasn't saving El. She knows how to swim. *She* was saving *him*!'

Lancelot listened, courteous and grave, then continued as if Stephen had never spoken. 'I knew you would want to meet the travellers, Sire. And I feel sure you will want to reward Lev for his bravery.'

'Indeed. But I perceive he is still soaked from his dunking in the river. He will take ill unless he change his clothes. You too, Lance. Off you go.' The king turned and crooked a finger at a man standing in the shadows behind him. 'Pray, Sir Kay, take Lev to my chamber and array him in my finest attire so that he is sensible of the honour in which we hold him.'

Meg hoped Stephen would volunteer to accompany them, to keep an eye on Lev, but he stayed silent, still sulking. She watched the three leave the room and felt a shiver of fear. Lev's fortunes were tied to their own. What if he betrayed them?

'You are cold.' Those keen eyes had caught her movement, but fortunately had misinterpreted it. King Arthur took Meg's hand and drew her closer to the fire. 'Come, warm yourself, Lady Margaret.' He kicked out at a large hound lying in front of the fireplace, blissfully toasting its belly. 'Move thyself, Cafal! Make way for the lady!'

At his master's touch, the dog leapt to his feet in a fluid ripple of muscles. He growled softly, showing large sharp teeth. Meg held out her hand to him, palm up, hoping he would understand her gesture of friendship. If not, he was large enough to take off her fingers.

'Nice dog,' she said hopefully.

Cafal came closer to investigate. He sniffed her hand, then gave her a slurpy lick. Greatly daring, Meg scratched his ears. The huge hound's eyes closed in ecstasy. He rubbed his body against her skirt.

Meg loved animals. She desperately wanted a pet. Her mum and dad worked such long hours in their shop, she hardly saw them. It was lonely at her house. Sure, she could chat to friends on the Internet, but she preferred to be with real people. That was why she spent so much time with El and Callie, and one of the reasons why she went to church — for the fellowship, for the feeling of belonging somewhere, being cared about and valued. She wished Cafal belonged to her. He'd make a wonderful companion.

A door opened, interrupting Meg's thoughts. A woman came in. She was smaller than anyone Meg had seen in Camelot, even though everyone seemed shorter than in the twenty-first century. The woman's eyes were a deep blue that was almost violet in the flickering light from the torches that illuminated the room. Her hair cascaded down her back in a cloud of shimmering gold. A heavy gold torc encircled her slim white neck, and she wore jewels in her ears and in the elaborately scrolled brooch at her breast. If Meg had believed in fairies, she might have thought this was one standing in front of them now. Even without the coronet circling her forehead, Meg could have guessed her identity from the way King Arthur welcomed her.

'My wife. Queen Guinevere.'

'Where is Lance?' She barely acknowledged the newcomers to the court.

'Changing his clothes. He attempted to save the Lady Elaine from drowning in the river, but failed. Fortunately, there was another who was successful. Lev. You will see Lance and Lev later, my dear, when they have changed out of their wet clothes.'

The queen's gaze flicked over El, and her mouth tightened in jealous appraisal. 'I am relieved Lance has come to no harm,' she said coolly.

'Your Majesty.' Lancelot hurried into the room, heading towards the queen like a homing pigeon. His eyes fixed on Guinevere's face as if seeking a sign, as if he was committing every beloved feature to memory. Meg felt a jolting pang of sympathy for Callie. Her task was a hopeless one, she felt certain of it. Why didn't the king say something? He must surely have noticed

Lancelot's infatuation? Perhaps he just didn't care, for he said only, 'We will talk further of these marvels while we feast. Will it please you to walk with me?'

He led them out and up a flight of stone stairs to the Great Hall. Meg paused with the others to wash her hands at a small, splashing fountain. The hall was as she remembered, but now there was life, movement. The room was lit by huge torches set in stone sconces, their flames leaping high, staining the air with smoke. Beneath their light knights mingled with the ladies, who looked bright as butterflies in their long silk dresses and glittering jewels.

The round table, Meg saw, was more of a hexagon — a series of long tables set in a round to accommodate all the guests at the feast. The acrid tang of smoke mingled with the rich scent of food as stewards laid out huge platters of meat, poultry and fish, and directed the more lowly servants who scuttled about their tasks. A tall, portly gentleman seemed to be directing proceedings. He raised a hand to salute the king as they entered the hall.

'Bedivere! You and Kay have excelled yourselves tonight!' King Arthur cuffed him lightly and moved on to take his place with the queen. The rest of the servants continued their work, ignoring King Arthur and his guests as if they didn't exist. Meg saw now why Stephen and El had come to the conclusion they were invisible in this land. The servants could see everyone all right, but did not call attention to their presence, nor did they speak to anyone.

At King Arthur's command, the assembly sat down at the table. Each knight had his own chair, with his name carved upon it, and a banner bearing his coat of arms floated behind. King Arthur's banner, with its huge red dragon, was the most splendid of them all. Ladies and other guests sat among the knights, each vying for the attention of their favourite.

The squires melted into the shadows behind, and the cup-bearers set about filling the coloured glass goblets with wine. Silver and gold platters sparkled in the flickering flames of the torches, their lustre echoed and refracted in the glowing colours of the jewels worn by the ladies. A large hourglass stood on one of the tables, slowly spilling the sands of time.

Meg could see no knives or forks and just a few spoons. Were they supposed to share? There were red pottery fingerbowls between each two settings, the water scented with floating rose petals. She glanced around, then reached out to the huge platter of fish set in front of her, to help herself with her fingers. She was stopped by the sound of King Arthur's voice as he recited a blessing. Squires hurried forward then, drawing their knives from their belts to carve the meats and fish for their knights and the ladies.

A movement across the table caught her eye. El had taken Lancelot's arm, demanding his attention. He listened politely, gave a brief reply, then turned back to Guinevere, who sat on his other side. Compared with the pale fragility of the queen, El seemed huge, tanned and muscular. Her mouth turned down in a sullen pout as she listened to the light banter passing between the knight and his queen.

Lev came in with Sir Kay. He wore a flowing scarlet cloak that almost covered a belted tunic and long breeches. Sir Kay was speaking and Lev looked bewildered. Meg strained to hear the conversation, but she could hear only snatches of talk about a vigil, a bath for purification and making confession. Sir Kay must be telling him about the ritual of becoming a knight.

The two of them sat down; Sir Kay next to King Arthur and Lev in the spare seat next to Stephen. Arthur immediately turned to engage Sir Kay in conversation, seeming oblivious of the attention Lancelot was showing Guinevere.

No wonder she fancied him more than the king! Meg hid a smile while she checked out Stephen and Lev. She'd hoped Stephen would keep an eye on Lev, but all his attention seemed to be focused on the knight sitting on his left, an older man with the ruddy complexion of someone who took his pleasure outdoors. Stephen must have forgotten his sulk over Lev's coming knighthood for he looked relaxed and cheerful. In fact, Meg had never seen him so animated as he laughed and talked, while the knight's squire helped the three of them to food.

She relaxed slightly as she saw Lev pick up a slice of the meat that had been placed on a piece of bread in front of him, and take a small bite. He must be feeling better. He took another mouthful, still using his fingers. Had he observed the company, or was that his usual style? He hunched over his food, guarding it carefully while he chewed, swallowed and took another bite. Then he noticed the goblet in front of him. He drank the wine down in a long series of swallows. His empty cup was immediately filled by one of the pages who circled the table, keeping a watchful eye on the guests. With a grunt, Lev drained its contents. It was refilled instantly. Meg hoped he wasn't going to get drunk. It would be awful if he was sick again. He swallowed, then wiped his mouth on his hand and hiccupped.

A snatch of conversation caught her attention: '... travelled back through time to be here.' Her eyes widened in horror as Stephen continued. 'We actually live in the twenty-first century — that's over two thousand years after Christ was born. We come from a country you don't know about because it hasn't been discovered yet. It's called Australia.'

Meg held her breath, waiting for the shout of discovery that there were devils and witches abroad, but the knight speared some more meat into his mouth and said calmly, 'Is your Astolat anywhere near the Perilous Forest, I wonder? We were there, Perceval, Galahad and I, on our search for the Holy Grail. Did you perhaps encounter there the devil who took a woman's form?'

'No! Er … no.'

The knight leaned forward. So did his squire. 'Her beauty tempted me from my pursuit of the Holy Grail. She set me against mine own brother so that we would have killed each other but for a voice that came from behind a cloud bidding me not to draw my sword. It was only when I turned to God for guidance that the devil woman was exposed in her true guise. But that was not the end of our adventures. I have fought a lion, a dragon and a leopard. I have even feasted from the Sangreal. Well I remember the time when …'

Meg tuned out then, acknowledging with a grin that any tale Stephen came up with was sure to be topped by his dinner companion.

A hungry grumble from her stomach drew her gaze downwards as the knight beside her carefully sliced a piece of bread and placed it in front of her. There were no empty plates on the tables; all the dishes were piled with food.

'Would you care for some salmon, lady?' The knight pointed his knife at the large whole fish, elaborately decorated with flowers and herbs, which lay in front of Meg. 'Or would you prefer venison? The king had success in the hunt today.' He gestured at a haunch of blackened meat.

Meg shuddered. 'Fish, thank you.' She studied him, caught by his dark good looks and the admiration in his warm brown eyes.

'Who are you? Pray tell me your name,' he asked.

'I am Meg.' She wasn't quite sure how to answer his question. Who was she anyway? A time traveller, lost in a strange place with people she didn't know and customs she didn't understand. She had no past here, no point of reference. It occurred to Meg that perhaps all migrants felt this way.

'Meg?' the knight queried.

'Lady Margaret.' Even her name was different here. She would have to reinvent herself, somehow find an identity.

I can be anyone I want, she thought. But who do I want to be? As she looked around the table, Meg acknowledged she was glad to be sitting here among the knights and their ladies. It was much better than being a castle servant, or the faggot-seller she'd seen earlier in the marketplace.

'Sir Mordred at your service, lady.' The knight beside her ducked his head in a brief bow, then began to slice the fish, expertly transferring part of it onto her piece of bread, and some onto his own.

'Mordred?' He wasn't in the least as she'd expected. 'King Arthur's son?' As soon as the words were out,

Meg wondered if she'd said the wrong thing. What if Mordred didn't know? What if Arthur preferred to keep their relationship a secret?

Surprise kept him silent for a moment. 'It appears that the news has travelled far and wide, lady,' he whispered then. 'It is true, but our kinship is not spoken of at court.' His smile had gone. Meg thought he was angry with her, until she read the unhappiness in his eyes.

'It worries you?' Meg picked up some fish in her fingers and transferred it to her mouth. She chewed and swallowed. The salmon was fresh and delicious.

Mordred hesitated. 'My aunt, Morgan le Fay, has seen into the future. She has seen dire things, terrible things that I cannot — must not — speak of.' He scowled at the food in front of him as he spoke. Their conversation seemed to have spoiled his appetite.

'There's going to be a battle? You're going to kill your father — King Arthur? Is that what she told you?'

'No! No! I cannot do it! I will not!' Mordred pushed away from the table. His chair grated against the rough flagstones, his action silencing the noise of laughter and conversation. Everyone stared at him. The king frowned a warning. Meg bent her head, angry with herself for provoking a scene. They were supposed to fit in, not cause trouble!

The low hum of conversation started again. Mordred leaned towards Meg, forcing her to look at him.

'Are you a fairy, lady?' he hissed. 'You see into the future?'

'I know something of it, yes,' Meg admitted.

'Then tell me Morgan and my mother are wrong! Tell me that my future is not tied up with Arthur's death. He is my father. He has been good to me. I honour and love him as much as any knight in this court.' His voice was passionate, despairing. Meg longed to comfort him.

'Causing his death may be told of as your destiny.' She thought of Callie's intention to change the outcome of the legend. Would she succeed? 'But what Morgan told you may not come to pass,' she continued. 'You see, where we come from we believe that people are responsible for what they do — that by their actions, they can sometimes change the future and create their own destiny.'

'But if it has been written? If fate decrees that I can be king only if I kill Arthur?'

'It is possible things may happen over which you have no control, which means your life may take a different path. You may never be put to the test.' She glanced at El sulking beside Lancelot and worry creased her forehead. If Callie planned to change the legend, it looked like she'd have to meet Lancelot herself. But in the meantime, Meg would do her bit to shake things up.

'Just remember, Mordred,' she urged. 'If you should

find yourself facing Arthur at Camlann, you don't have to fight him. You could throw down your sword and leave the battlefield. You could even refuse to go to battle in the first place.'

'And lose my honour along with my sword?' Mordred shook his head. 'Nay lady, we do not live by your sort of code, not at this court. We are knights, bound together by chivalry and brotherhood.' He looked down the table at Lancelot. Hatred and envy blazed suddenly in his eyes. But then his gaze moved on to Guinevere with a look of hopeless longing. Meg felt a chill. By the time they met at Camlann, perhaps Mordred would be ready to kill his father in order to marry his queen.

'The Breton forgets himself and his loyalty to the king!' Mordred hissed. There was no mistaking who he meant. No mistaking, either, the venom in his voice.

Meg searched frantically for a safer topic of conversation. She remembered the question that had intrigued her earlier. 'I have heard talk of the Mother Goddess. Is the court Christian or pagan?' she asked.

Mordred blinked. 'The court is Christian. Those who still followed the old ways quickly chose the White Christ when the time came to go in search of the Holy Grail. And we defend ourselves under the cross in battle, so that we are not mistaken for the barbarians.'

'And you?' Meg thought of his aunt Morgan and his

belief in her prophecy. 'Which god, or goddess, do you worship?'

Mordred sighed. 'My family has always followed the old ways,' he said obliquely.

Meg had finished the salmon Mordred had given her. Still hungry, she picked up the slice of bread on which the fish rested and was just about to take a bite when Mordred grasped her arm. 'The trencher is not for us, lady. It will be given to the poor to eat, along with our scraps, after we have feasted.'

She dropped the bread quickly, feeling stupid, and Mordred placed on it a blackened slice of meat, smelling of herbs and charcoal. She glanced down the length of the table. 'Are there any vegetables?' she asked.

'Vegetables?' Mordred echoed. 'Only the poor eat vegetables.' He took a sip of wine, while Meg pushed away the slice of bread and meat.

'May I have some more salmon?' she asked.

'Of course.' Mordred cut off a second slice of bread, piled some salmon on it, and placed it in front of her.

'Thank you.' She ate hungrily.

'And where are you lodging in Camelot?'

'We're staying in the tower.' Meg's voice was muffled. She swallowed hastily. 'I thought it was supposed to be on an island?' She washed the salmon down with several sips of wine.

Mordred smiled. 'It becomes an island when the

rains come hard and the river bursts its banks. Sometimes the tower is cut off from us for several moons.'

He raised the enamelled wine pitcher and refilled their goblets. Meg had another drink, wishing it was water. She was already feeling light-headed, but the fish was making her thirsty.

'I have heard tell there is a fairy lives there, weaving magic webs and singing faerie songs.'

'Yes.' Meg smiled, thinking there was no need for telephones in Camelot. 'But Callie — Charlotte — is not a fairy. She's our sister.'

'Why is she not here with you tonight? Is she under enchantment to stay locked up in the tower?'

Not knowing what else to say, Meg nodded.

'The Island of Charlotte.' Mordred nodded thoughtfully. 'No-one has lived there for many years.'

'There are heaps of servants there,' Meg protested, remembering the food Stephen and El had brought back from their exploration.

'Yes, of course.' Mordred dismissed them with an airy wave of his hand. 'They keep food on the table in case the lord and his lady should return unexpectedly. But they fled the tower many moons ago, after Morgan put a curse on it.'

'Why did she do that?'

'Oh.' Mordred shook his head, his face darkening to misery. ''Twas said that a lady would come there who would bewitch one of the king's court; who might change the destiny Morgan foretold for me.'

Callie! Isn't that what you want? Meg thought as she finished her wine. It was sweet and refreshing.

Mordred tipped the jug and poured her some more. 'I am Arthur's heir. It is my right to be king. But I would rather have Arthur's blessing than cause his death,' he said quietly as he refilled his own goblet. 'But Morgan won't heed me. She and my mother Morgause have high ambition, and they are impatient. There is nought anyone can do to break the spells they have woven and the prophecy they have foretold.'

Meg shook her head. Obviously Mordred believed what his aunt had told him. But had he looked into his own heart and seen the true reason for his fate?

She tried another tack. 'I have told you that I can see into the future, and I tell you now that both you and Arthur will die if you fight at Camlann. You will never inherit Camelot.'

'If my fate is to be slain by Arthur, then I must die with honour.' Mordred took up his goblet and drained its contents, as if trying to block the future from his mind.

'You must ask for a treaty instead,' Meg urged, remembering what Ms Hope had told them. 'And before you meet at Camlann, send beaters across the field looking for snakes. Kill them all. Even that might be enough to save Camelot.'

Mordred looked at Meg in admiration. 'Truly, I believe you see the future, lady. I shall do as you say.'

'But it may never come to that. Despite your aunt's tricks there's a lady in the tower now. Our sister, Charlotte. So maybe the prophecy will fail?' She hoped for both Mordred's and Callie's sake that she might be right.

'That is so,' Mordred acknowledged. 'It may well turn out that whatever comes between us may be solved with honour and without bloodshed.'

He smiled then, seeming to relax as he sat back to enjoy the performances of the musicians and the acrobats who tumbled into the hall to entertain them.

With the sun long gone the air was chill, but Callie did not dare go to the window to close it. Once more she glanced at the mirror. It remained dark and empty. Everything was quiet, and for one crazy moment she wondered if she was the only one alive in Camelot. Was she even in Camelot? Maybe she was really at home, imagining everything that was going on?

She sat very still, listening intently. The rats, unseen now, scuffled and squeaked. They were definitely alive. Then, from far below, she heard the faint sound of voices. She felt slightly comforted. Help was at hand, if necessary. She wondered what was happening at home. Gran must have realised by now that they were gone. Maybe she'd already spoken to Dad, urging him to come home to Australia. There could well be a full-scale search in progress. Callie imagined her father going into his workroom and finding the computer. Had it blown up, or was her program still there? Would he realise what had happened? Would he be able to come after them and rescue them? Or, angry at her interference and not realising they were lost in Camelot, would he simply delete the program and send them all into oblivion?

With an effort she brought her thoughts back to her present predicament. Where were the others? She wondered what time it was now, here in Camelot? It felt very late. She was tired. Exhausted. But she dared not go to bed. What if the others never came back? What if she fell asleep and never woke up again? What if the rats came out and ran all over her while she was sleeping?

She pressed her hand tight against the thudding beat of her frightened heart. She'd go mad if she carried on like this. It was better to think about Camelot. And Lancelot. And Guinevere. Had the others gone up to check out the court and all the people in it? What were they doing? How were they getting on?

CHAPTER EIGHT

eg finished the last of her third helping of salmon and sat back, pushing away the piece of bread that had served as her plate. She felt pleasantly full and slightly sleepy after the wine she'd drunk. Pages began to clear the table, to make way for the next course: platters of cakes, pastries, fruits and nuts.

She looked down the length of the table. Mordred had been captured in conversation by the lady on his other side. No-one was looking at her. Hating what she had to do, especially after being warned off by him, she reached out to the slab of meat that Mordred had placed on the hunk of bread. Hastily, she rolled it up like a doner kebab. It was chunky, oozing juices, but it was the best she could do. She couldn't return to the tower empty-handed, while boasting of the feast they had attended — not when Callie had been left all alone with only the lunchtime scraps to eat.

Meg slipped the messy bundle into the purse hanging from her girdle. She hoped they could leave before meat juices leaked onto her skirt.

But the meal was not over yet. Boden entered, balanced on his stilts, to tell jokes and stories of his travels. A jongleur sang songs of lusty deeds and unrequited love while jugglers, wrestlers and acrobats performed feats of skill and daring.

Suddenly a voice rose above the quiet chatter of the guests. 'I feel sick. I gotta get outta here.'

Horrified, Meg leaned across the table, trying to shush Lev. Stephen grabbed him by the arm. He shook Lev and muttered something in a low, urgent undertone. Several of the guests had heard Lev and were looking at him instead of the performers. Meg closed her eyes, waiting for King Arthur to lose his temper and throw them out.

A shout from further down the table drew everyone's eyes away from Lev. A knight staggered to his feet, gasping and choking. He clutched at his throat and fought for breath, but even as Meg watched, his face turned purple and he fell to the floor, dropping the half-eaten apple he held in his hand.

'Sir Patrise!' King Arthur pushed back his chair and hurried to the fallen figure. But El had got there first. She fell to her knees beside the knight, doubling him over and whacking him hard on the back in case he had a piece of apple stuck in his throat. But he had stopped breathing.

She shoved a finger in his mouth then, hooking his tongue out of the way, seeking the blockage. But the airway was clear. Frowning, she bent over the knight and started mouth-to-mouth.

'Kissing him will not bring him back to life, lady.' King Arthur knelt beside El.

'I'm not kissing him!' El panted between breaths. 'I'm trying to save his life!' She thumped the knight's chest hard — once, twice — then again placed her lips over his.

''Tis no use. I fear Sir Patrise is dead.'

El stopped to look at the blue lips and contorted face of the knight. She felt his wrist for a pulse, but found none. Slowly, she stood up.

King Arthur crossed himself, then snapped his fingers. 'Sir Kay!'

The portly knight bustled forward, followed by several of the other knights. Together, they carried Sir Patrise from the Great Hall. Their exit left a subdued hush.

'Your sister was brave to do what she did,' Mordred commented. 'Some poison might have been transferred from Sir Patrise's lips to her own when she tried to save him with her breath.'

'Poison?' Meg was horrified.

'Indeed.' Mordred sounded troubled. 'Sir Kay, the king's seneschal, was in charge of organising the feast this night. Someone will have to be called to account for what has happened.'

'No! I don't believe it. He choked to death, that's all.' It was vital that Mordred believe her — that they all did. Because if it was poison, if there was any trouble at court, then surely the newcomers would be the first to come under suspicion?

Mordred shook his head. 'I know the signs. And if it is proven, then blame must fall on the one who ordered the preparation of this feast.'

Meg didn't need to ask who Mordred suspected. His grim, unhappy face as he stared at the queen told her all she needed to know.

'Perhaps the apple was meant for the king?' he whispered, the words so soft Meg wasn't sure she'd heard him properly. She felt a chill of foreboding.

With the body of Sir Patrise gone, King Arthur beckoned the rest of his guests to leave the table. Stephen dragged Lev to his feet. The knight beside him came to help, taking Lev's other arm. Lev straightened and wiped his nose. He was sweating badly. 'I don't feel so good. I've gotta pain in me gut.'

Meg hurried to his side. 'It's Meg, Lev. Do you

remember me?' she whispered, detaching Lev from Stephen and the knight, and drawing him away. 'Something's happened to us. We've come back in time to another place. To Camelot. Do you understand what I'm saying?'

'Yeah, okay. If you say so.' Lev shivered as he clutched his stomach.

Stephen came up beside Meg and grabbed Lev. 'Don't give us any trouble.' He gave Lev a shake, then noticed that his table companion had followed him and was watching closely. Hurriedly, he dropped Lev's arm. 'This is Sir Bors de Ganis. And this is Howell,' he added as the young squire stepped closer.

'Lady Margaret,' said Meg. El hurried up to them, flushed and out of breath after her attempt to save Sir Patrise. 'And the Lady Elaine.'

'I am at your service, ladies.' Bors bowed, then turned to El. 'I am sorry you could not help Sir Patrise, but it was well done, lady.'

El looked a little happier.

'We shall have the ceremony to knight Lev tomorrow morning.' King Arthur walked towards them. Instinctively, Meg stepped in front of Lev, trying to hide him.

'You must make preparation tonight,' Arthur continued, drawing Lev forward. 'You must make your vows to Christ.'

'Huh?' Lev gaped at him.

Meg racked her brains, frantic to come up with a reason to change the king's mind.

'Lancelot will accompany you to the chapel tonight and will pray with you in preparation for your coming honour,' King Arthur continued.

'Yeah, right,' Lev mumbled.

'Sire! Your Majesty.' Meg wasn't sure how to address Arthur but thought somebody should. The sooner they got Lev back to the tower, the better. No way could they let him loose with Lancelot. 'I fear Lev has taken ill after the dunking he received in the river. Perhaps the ceremony may wait a little longer?'

'Tomorrow we hold a tourney — the joust for the ninth diamond. It is my wish that there be a new knight at court to take part in the contest.' King Arthur's face was slightly flushed; it was clear he wasn't used to having his judgment questioned.

'But Sire …'

'After the tragedy tonight, we need a diversion,' Arthur said firmly.

'Then may I accompany him, Sire?' Someone would have to stay with Lev, Meg thought, but the others should go back to the tower, to reassure Callie they hadn't dropped off the face of the earth. El couldn't go on her own. Stephen would have to escort her, though Meg would rather have had him here to help look after Lev.

'You may stay with him, if you wish.' But King

Arthur still looked displeased. He turned to the others. 'I hope you will accept lodging here in the castle?'

'No,' El said quickly, before Meg could speak. 'Thank you, Sire, but our sister is alone in the tower and we must return to her.' She turned towards Meg. 'You too.'

'I can't just abandon —'

'Bors, send your squire to escort the travellers back to the tower. For their protection,' King Arthur interrupted. Not waiting for a reply, he turned on his heel and rejoined the queen who lingered, waiting for him and Lancelot. The king muttered a few words to Lancelot, then led the rest of the entourage out of the Great Hall, pausing to wash his hands once more.

El frowned, as angry as Arthur at having her judgment questioned and angry too that it would be Meg staying with Lancelot for the night. 'Bring Lev back as soon as you can,' she said. She picked up her skirt and flounced off.

But Meg had no intention of letting El leave just yet. She raced after her, not caring if it offended court etiquette or not. 'Food for Callie!' She pulled the kebab out of her purse and thrust it into El's hand.

'Good thinking, Meg. I wanted to take something, but I couldn't work out how to do it.' El shoved the leaking bundle into her own purse.

'Lady Margaret!' Lancelot called, beckoning her to follow him. One hand rested lightly on Lev's shoulder, in his other hand he held a flaming torch to illuminate their journey. Meg came up beside them and clasped Lev's elbow in case he needed support. Irritably, he shrugged her off.

'Lead on,' said Meg, wondering where their journey would take them and how the night would end.

As they left the walled city of Camelot and set off across the fields, Stephen hummed a tune under his breath.

'You sound happy,' El commented sourly.

At once, Stephen stopped humming. It was true, he thought, surprised that he felt as cheerful as he did under the circumstances. He wondered if his parents were worried about him, and decided he didn't care. He really was happy, he realised. The weight of responsibility had lifted from his shoulders and for the first time since he could remember, he felt strong and confident in his ability to be himself and explore what he wanted from life.

He shot a quick glance at Howell, who held a large flaming torch in his hand to light their way through the dark night. The light caught the sharp angles of Howell's cheekbones and turned his eyes into dark, empty sockets. But then Howell turned and smiled at him. The gleam of reflected lamplight brought life shining to his eyes. Stephen returned his smile, feeling its warmth flow through his body.

'I had a good time tonight,' he said, chuckling as he recalled the tall tales of his table companion. His tongue loosened by the wine he'd consumed, Stephen had boasted of home and life in twenty-first century Australia to Bors, and to Howell who had stood close behind them, listening carefully. 'We have aeroplanes that fly us from country to country. We even have spaceships that fly to the moon and to other planets.'

'That's nothing,' Bors had countered. 'Galahad, Perceval and I travelled on a magical ship built by King Solomon.' With frequent interruptions from his squire, he'd gone on to regale Stephen with more tales of his own exploits during their search for the Holy Grail, seeming to take it as a matter of pride that his stories sounded far more fantastic than anything Stephen could come up with.

'You have to help me persuade Callie to stay in the tower and get us home,' El said, breaking into his reverie.

'Why?'

'Why?' El stopped dead. 'Don't you want to go home?'

Stephen felt a stab of anger that El would speak their secrets in front of Howell, as if he didn't matter. He glanced at Bors' squire and felt the same lift of happiness he'd experienced before. He'd found out that Howell was a few years older than himself. Like Stephen, he was hoping to be knighted although, unlike Stephen, he was still unsure of his worth.

He was short and slender; a dark Celt who often used words unfamiliar to Stephen although he could guess their meaning well enough. There was an easy familiarity between him and Bors. Stephen envied them that. He'd never known that sort of friendship. 'I'm not in any hurry to leave Camelot,' he said.

'You can't mean it!' El started walking again, her mouth twisted in angry frustration.

'Why are you in such a hurry? Why can't you wait until Callie meets Lancelot? That's why she's here.'

'She can't meet him! She'll die if she leaves the tower. That's what it says in the legend.'

'You don't believe all that guff, do you?'

'It's too much of a risk.'

'Why don't you bring Lancelot to the tower, then? Let him come to Callie instead?'

'But …' But El didn't want to admit that she wanted Lancelot for herself, if only to prove to Callie that she could get him. 'It's too much of a risk letting Callie see him,' she blustered.

'You can't watch out for her forever, you know. Sooner or later she's got to lead her own life.'

'But she's hopeless on her own! She needs me to take care of her.'

'Really?'

El flushed, knowing Stephen didn't believe her, even though she'd meant what she'd said. 'I hate this place!'

she burst out, remembering Lancelot's neglect of her during the meal. 'I don't know how to behave. I don't know what to do.'

'You knew what to do for that dead knight.'

'It didn't help.'

'No, but at least you tried. It was more than anyone else did.'

El was silenced by the compliment. She didn't get many, although she tried constantly to do the right thing and be better than anyone else, including Callie.

Stephen smiled to himself in the darkness. 'Callie must be very clever to have worked out the program that brought us back in time to this place,' he said, enjoying having El at a disadvantage.

'Yes, she is,' El admitted. After a pause she added, 'Actually, she's my father's favourite. She's just like my mother, you see.'

'But you're almost identical.'

'Not in character. I'm more practical, like my dad. My mother was an artist, like Callie.'

'Was?'

'Is.' Not wanting Stephen to get the wrong idea, El continued, 'She shot through six years ago. She told Dad she was going up north to join an artists' colony, to devote herself to art and to find herself as a person. But Dad doesn't believe that; he thinks she went off with someone. I know, cos he told me once after he'd had a row with Callie. He's terrified she's going to chase after our mother, that he'll lose her if he lets her study art. He never talks about Mum, at least not to Callie. Only to me, cos he knows I'll never do what Mum did.'

There was a note of self-righteous satisfaction in El's voice that annoyed Stephen, but he said only, 'You must miss her.'

'No, I don't. We're better off without her. She was always wrapped up in her own life anyway.' El trudged along silently for some moments. 'Even if he won't admit it, I think Dad misses her,' she said then, adding, 'And so does Callie.'

Stephen wondered what it would feel like to miss your parents. He didn't, not at all. But he thought Meg might. He wondered how she was getting on.

'This way.' Lancelot unbolted the wooden door and guided Lev and Meg into the small stone chapel. His torch flamed bright in the still, dank air, illuminating the scene. He fixed it into a niche in the wall, then kneeled to face the altar and genuflected. Hastily Meg copied his movements, then nudged Lev.

Irritated, he shoved a bony elbow into her side.

'The priest will hear your confession now.' Lancelot grasped Lev's arm, ready to lead him to the confessional.

'Confession?' Lev gave a low grating laugh. He coughed, and then wiped the back of his hand across his nose. 'What am I supposed to say?'

'You can ask God to help you,' Meg prompted.

'I don't need God's help. What I need is somewhere to live, a job, and enough money to take care of meself.'

'You have no home?' Lancelot sounded horrified.

'Not where we come from.' Too late, Meg remembered they were supposed to be brother and sister. 'But I'm sure we can work something out,' she called after Lev as Lancelot led him towards the priest.

She watched as Lev slumped to his knees and the priest began his blessing. Was God listening? Would they ever get home? And if they did, would Lev find the courage and help he needed to turn his life around?

Meg said a quick prayer of her own, and then looked about her. Webs of stone ribbing threaded the arched vaults above her head, lending support to the domed ceiling. The walls were decorated with carvings of saints, and intersected by stained-glass windows. It was too dark to see what the scenes depicted, but the flickering torchlight caught glimmering flashes of gold, ruby, peacock blue and emerald green. Slowly, she walked along the flagged nave towards the altar. There were no pews to sit on, so she knelt down on the hard stone floor and folded her hands once more in prayer.

It was cold and the air smelt stale, tainted with

the memory of unwashed bodies and damp wool, and overlaid by the elusive fragrance of something spicy. Incense? Lancelot came and joined her. He sank to his knees and began to recite a prayer in what sounded like Latin. Meg bent her head, unable to join in but thinking she should find something to say.

This church was so different from the cheerful good humour of the church she attended, where God seemed so accessible and forgiving. The Pentecostal church was more like a theatre, with its rows of coloured plastic seats, the stage in front lit by flood-lights, the video cameras set at strategic points to record the pastor's words and the music and singing of the band and choir. She'd never been in a church like this before, somewhere so ancient, so austere, so holy.

A shuffle of feet caught her attention. She looked over her shoulder as a file of black-robed monks formed a line down one side of the chapel. They must have come to keep vigil with Lev.

A strong, deep voice led the chorus:

'*Miserere mei Deus: secundum magnam misericordiam tuam …*'

Meg caught her breath, transfixed as other voices joined in, giving body and texture to the music:

'*Amplius lava me ab iniquitate mea: et a peccato meo munda me …*'*

Suddenly the high clear notes of a boy soprano soared above the chorus. Meg didn't understand the words but the sound sent a shiver of delight down her spine. So penitent. So reverent. The music was stark, simple; utterly beautiful.

They were all singing now — a full-throated chorus of supplication. For the first time Meg saw God as a being greater than herself: not a friend but a presence both mystical and terrifying. She felt humble and afraid. 'Oh God, hear me,' she prayed quietly. 'Help me. Help us …'

To do what? It seemed presumptuous to ask for anything in this holy place. But as she listened to the music, she felt her fear subside. In its place came acceptance of whatever might lie ahead. And with acceptance came peace.

'I kept vigil with my own son before he was knighted.' Lancelot's voice disturbed her thoughts. He rubbed his hands together and blew on his fingers for warmth.

'Galahad?' Meg wondered why Lancelot sounded so sad.

'You have heard of him, then? He was a fine knight, the bravest and best of all.' There was pride as well as sorrow in Lancelot's voice.

Meg hesitated as curiosity fought with not wanting to pry. Curiosity won. 'What became of him?'

'He went in search of the Holy Grail, the Sangreal,

along with many knights from Camelot. But only Galahad, Bors and Perceval were pure enough to find the Grail and partake of its magical properties. Galahad fulfilled the ancient prophecy: he cured the Fisher King of his wounds and restored life to the Waste Forest.' Lancelot bent his head. 'I myself was not worthy ...' Meg wondered if he was thinking of Guinevere, if he felt ashamed of his liaison with her.

'... but my son proved himself a chaste and honest knight, worthy of the great honour bestowed upon him.'

'What happened to him after he found the Grail?'

'He died.' Lancelot crossed himself, then pressed a thumb across his eyes, surreptitiously wiping away tears. 'After that, Perceval left for a hermitage. He took a vow of silence, and died a year later. He is buried alongside his sister and Galahad. Bors arranged the funeral before he returned here to Camelot.' Lancelot was silent for a moment. Then he said savagely, 'Sometimes I wish ...' He stopped, reconsidering his outburst.

'What do you wish?' Meg prompted.

Lancelot cleared his throat. 'May God forgive me for saying so, but I wish we had never seen the Grail, never followed it. We forgot our duty here at court, and found shame and humiliation instead. We lost so many of our best and bravest knights in its pursuit. Our court will never be as strong and united again. And I lost my son … my son …' He bowed his head, hiding his anguish. Once more, his lips moved in prayer.

Lev came over then and joined them at the altar. Meg stole a sideways glance as he slumped onto the stone floor. He was still sweating heavily; he gave a low groan as he rubbed his legs, trying to relieve the cramps that tormented him. He seemed strangely subdued. She wondered what the priest had said to him.

'Tunc acceptabis sacrificium justitiae
oblationes and holocausta:
tunc imponent super altare tuum vitulos.' **

The music ceased. The monks quietly shuffled out. Meg wondered what would happen next. She shifted uncomfortably, hoping they wouldn't have to stay kneeling all night. 'I know nothing of the ritual of knighthood. Can you tell me about it?' she asked, thinking that the knowledge might help both her and Lev.

Lancelot rose and shook himself, as if freeing his mind from the memories that tormented him. He took her hand to help her up, then led them both to the far side of the chapel. Meg stamped her feet, prickled by pins and needles as blood circulated freely through her legs once more. The stone floor had been hard and cold on her knees. Perhaps people developed calluses and an alternative circulation pattern if they came here regularly for Mass. She crossed her arms, hugging herself, and shivered.

'Now that Lev has taken confession and been blessed, he must wash himself clean of all sin.'

For Lev's sake, Meg hoped that the bath would be hot. She wondered if she could ask for one too.

'He will sleep through the rest of the night in a new bed with clean white sheets. In the morning I will help him dress in a white robe, to signify cleanliness, and a scarlet cloak that reminds the knight of his duty to shed his blood in defence of God and the church. He will put on brown stockings to remind him of the earth to which he will return after death. And he will be given a belt of white, signifying virginity and to remind him to guard against lust.'

Meg's mouth quivered up in a smile.

'What's this knighthood stuff all about?' Lev sniffed, and wiped his nose on his sleeve. Lancelot looked askance.

'Don't you remember? You saved El from drowning,' Meg said quickly.

'Eh?' Lev looked puzzled. So did Lancelot.

'Can you not remember your heroic deeds? Have you a chill? Have your wits been addled?' Concerned, he laid a hand on Lev's shoulder.

'Nuh, I'm good. I'm right.' Lev brushed him off impatiently.

'I am pleased to hear you say so.' Lancelot took him literally. 'You may become a knight only if you are truly repentant and in a state of grace.'

Meg grinned. Hastily she raised a hand to her mouth to hide her amusement. What had Lev told the priest during confession? Had he been absolved from his sins?

'You will be given golden spurs to urge you to follow God's commandments; and a sharp sword with two keen edges to remind you that justice and loyalty go hand in hand, and that it is the knight's task to defend the poor and oppressed,' Lancelot continued. 'Finally, King Arthur will touch your shoulder with the sword Excalibur, and you will be told of the four commandments by which a knight must live: not to consent to false judgment or commit treason, to honour and protect all women and damsels, to hear Mass every day and to fast every Friday in memory of Christ's passion.'

Lev's shivering was growing worse. Great shudders shook his body at intervals. He leaned over and growled, 'You've gotta help me. I feel really bad.' With a low moan, he collapsed at Meg's feet.

'He's not well.' Meg cast a glance of appeal at Lancelot. 'Is there perhaps some herbal potion …?'

'Of course. I shall seek physic from the infirmarium to help Lev pass a peaceful night.' Lancelot cast a worried glance at the shivering, shaking figure slumped in front of him. 'Perhaps I should rather seek the help of Nimue? Or even Morgan herself?'

Meg's eyes widened. A meeting with the High Priestess of Magic! That really would be something.

'But no.' Lancelot shook his head as he answered his own question. 'Lev has been purified. We cannot turn to the old ways now.' He stepped quickly to the open door of the chapel. 'Wait with him until I return. I shall not be long,' he called over his shoulder.

Meg knelt beside Lev, wincing as her sore knees grated on the hard stone flagging. She bent her ear to his mouth and was relieved to hear a faint, sighing breath. 'Wake up!' She shook him, anxious not to waste any more time. Reluctantly, he opened one eye and stared blearily at her. Then he heaved himself to a sitting position and doubled over, nursing his stomach.

'Cramps,' he gasped. 'Help me.'

'Lancelot's gone to fetch something to take away the pain.' Meg sat back and felt Lev's forehead once more. His skin burned under her fingers. No wonder he was so out of it. His temperature was way too high. 'While Lancelot's gone, there's something I have to explain to you,' she continued. 'Please listen carefully, Lev. It's important that you understand what's happened so you don't get us all in trouble.'

She told Lev all about Callie's program and why they were in Camelot. As she spoke, the music of the monks threaded through her thoughts: the intricate melody; the clear, pure voice of the boy soprano. Meg made a silent vow that if they ever got back to their own time, she would find out more about this ancient music that seemed to echo the very harmony of the universe. She might even try to create her own.

*'Have mercy upon me, O God: according to thy loving kindness ... Wash me thoroughly from mine iniquity, and cleanse me from my sin.

**Then shalt thou be pleased with the sacrifice of righteousness, with the burnt offerings and oblations; then shall they offer young bullocks upon thine altar.'

Psalm 51

CHAPTER NINE

Lev stretched out on the soft mattress, feeling the slight prickle of feather quills against his skin. Everything hurt. There was the sour taste of sickness in his mouth. He moistened his lips with his tongue, remembering the drink Lancelot had brought him. 'Syrup of poppies to ease the pain and help you sleep.' Lancelot had supported his head, making sure he drank every honeysweet drop of it. It had tasted like lolly water and it wasn't helping.

He closed his eyes, trying to sort out what Meg had told him. When they'd first arrived he'd been too sick to make much sense of all those knights and the king and queen and everything. He'd thought he must be on some sort of movie set. But Meg had said it was real; that they'd travelled back in time to Camelot, to the court of King Arthur, and now they were stuck here. He could hardly believe it — especially the bit about being knighted. That was what all the praying and chanting was about. Meg had told him he'd been brave, had rescued someone from drowning.

Sweating under the fur blanket, Lev felt his flesh creep as he remembered being dragged into the river, the shock of icy water closing over his head.

Confused images came to him: someone pushing his head under water, trying to drown him. Lancelot plunging into the river with his armour on. People splashing and shouting. Him clinging onto someone, a lifeline to the river bank. He remembered being hoisted onto Lancelot's horse, and the long agonising ride into Camelot. But he couldn't remember being brave, or being anything other than scared and angry, just as he had been all his life.

But he'd saved someone from drowning. For the first time in his life, it seemed he'd done something good. And it must be true, because he was going to be knighted for it. Tomorrow, he'd be Sir Lev, one of the knights of the Round Table.

The pain was easing now and he was starting to feel sleepy. As he let himself drift off into darkness, Lev felt something he'd never felt before: pride. Maybe he was worth something after all. Maybe, once he was knighted, everyone would treat him differently. Everyone? Who was here with him? Apart from Meg and Lancelot, he couldn't really remember. 'Stephen,' she'd said. Was that the tall, fair-haired guy who'd tried to drown him? And El? She was the twin to Callie who'd messed with her dad's program and brought them back to Camelot. El was the one he was supposed to have saved from drowning. She looked like the other girl, the one who'd been kind to him at school. Callie?

'Where have you been? I've been out of my mind worrying about you.' Callie flew to the door as soon as she heard the latch snick. Full of anger and self-pity, she faced her sister and Stephen. 'I've had a horrible night. There're rats all over the place and I ...' Concerned, she leaned past them to check out the shadows beyond the doorway. 'Who's this? And where are Meg and Lev? What's happened to them?'

'They're safe. But it's a long story.' El thrust the rolled kebab at her sister. 'Sit down and eat this,' she said, 'and I'll tell you all about it.'

'Callie, this is Howell, Sir Bors de Ganis's squire,' said Stephen. Callie nodded at the dark youth, questions in her eyes. Stephen smiled at Howell. 'Thanks for walking back with us,' he said.

'It was my duty and also my pleasure.' Howell bowed to them all. 'I hope to see you tomorrow at the tournament.'

'We'll come if we can.' El answered for everyone.

'I'm sorry we've been gone so long,' said Stephen as Howell clattered off down the stairs. 'We met up with Lancelot while we were out swimming. We went with him to Camelot. And Lev is to be made a knight.'

'You met Lancelot?' Focusing on what mattered most to her, Callie ignored the aggressive tone in Stephen's voice.

'You're right, Callie. He's really cute.'

Callie shot a sharp glance at her sister.

'And we've decided the best thing is to bring him to the tower. To you,' said Stephen. 'We'll go to Camelot for the ceremony tomorrow morning, and bring Meg and Lev back with us as well as Lancelot.'

Reassured by their presence, and by Stephen's words, Callie slumped onto a chair and took a bite of the kebab. She felt too tired and too tense to eat, but picked at it as El spilled out the story, with interruptions from Stephen, of their adventures in the river and at Camelot. By the time she'd finished, Callie was almost asleep.

'I'm going to crash next door.' Stephen stood up and yawned widely. 'Good night.'

Callie pulled off her dress and hung it over the pole beside the bed, then flopped into the large four-poster bed beside El. 'You've gotta stay awake … keep the rats away.' She was asleep almost before she closed her eyes.

'Yeah, yeah, yeah,' El mumbled. But they both slept the deep sleep of exhaustion. They saw and heard nothing of their nocturnal visitors.

'Wake up! We've come to fetch you for the tournament,' Meg sang out.

'Wha … What?' El opened one eye, sleepily pushing her hair off her face so that she could see. As she sat up in bed and blearily took in her surroundings, memory returned and she groaned.

'Let me introduce you to Sir Lavaine,' Meg laughed, stepping aside and shoving Lev forward.

'Lavaine?' Callie sat up with a jerk.

'That's what King Arthur said when he dubbed him a knight: "Arise, Sir Lavaine." I guess he thought Lev wasn't a proper name for a knight. Is Lavaine your real name, Lev?'

'Dunno.' Lev shrugged, his lips quirking up in a smile of satisfaction at the memory of the ceremony. He stroked the rough chain mail of his new armour, reassuring himself that it was real. Lancelot had given him more lolly water before the ceremony. He was feeling really good now. Confident. Proud. Determined to do his best to fit into his new role.

'This is El. And Callie.' Meg pointed at each twin in turn. 'Do you remember them?'

'Yeah. I know you from school.' Lev peered from Callie to El. 'Twins.'

'Well done!' El said, her voice edged with sarcasm.

Lev took it as a compliment. 'You look the same. Which one of you did I save?'

'You wish.' El snorted.

'I didn't save anyone?'

'Of course not.' Her look withered his new-found confidence. 'You damn near drowned. I saved *you*!'

'So why was I knighted?'

'Because the boobies in this century don't believe women are capable of doing anything except flirting and swooning and stupid things like that.'

Lev gaped at El.

'But now you've been made a knight, you must try to live up to it,' Meg interposed tactfully. 'We could all be in trouble if they find out who and what we really are.'

'You want me to live a lie? Pretend to be something I'm not?' Lev looked absolutely shattered.

'Better a knight than a reject from the streets,' El retorted.

Lev glared at her, wishing he could wipe that smug expression off her face.

'Did you bring Lancelot back with you?' Callie was

more interested in Stephen's promise than Lev's shattered illusions.

'No. It's been one helluva morning, actually. There's so much to tell you,' said Meg.

'Just wait till I get Stephen.' El hopped out of bed and, not bothering to dress, ran out of the room in her shift.

'Stephen!' She banged on the door opposite their own, then walked straight in and pushed back the drapes of the bed. 'Hurry! Meg and Lev are back. There's to be a tournament and we're going.'

Stephen woke from a dream. He'd been walking through the fields with El in the moonlight, just as they'd walked last night. Only this time he'd put his hands on El's shoulders, and kissed her. And she'd laughed at him. Now she was right here, looking down at him. Could she tell what he'd been dreaming?

'Be with you in a minute,' he croaked.

'Okay.' To his relief, El hurried out, not waiting for him to get out of bed.

He threw on his clothes and hurried across to the girls' room. Trying to seem casual, although he still felt embarrassed, he propped himself against the table. 'What's going on?' he asked.

El had already hopped back into bed beside Callie.

'Lancelot's shot through. Sorry to be the bearer of bad news.' Meg went on to explain. 'Remember that knight you tried to save last night, El? Well, it seems he was poisoned, and the story got around that Guinevere was to blame but that she got the wrong guy. There are whispers of treason. They're saying that she actually tried to kill the king so that she and Lancelot would be free to marry.'

'What?' Callie's face drained of colour. Her knuckles showed white as she clutched the fur blanket tightly to her chest.

'It's all been denied,' Meg said hastily. 'But there was a duel this morning. Lancelot defended the queen's honour against Sir Mador, who's related to Sir Patrise, the dead knight. Bors was going to fight Sir Mador at first, but Lancelot insisted that his reputation was at stake just as much as the queen's, so he fought him instead. No-one was killed, but Lancelot left straight afterwards. He didn't even wait for Lev to be knighted.'

'Where's Lancelot gone?' Callie was almost in tears. She couldn't believe she'd come so close, only to fail now.

Meg shrugged. 'He's lying low till the heat dies down, I suppose.'

'Then I'm going after him.' Callie threw back the covers and hopped out of bed. Then she paused. 'What is this tournament? What's it about?'

'It's the joust for the ninth diamond. Lancelot has won the other eight diamonds already. He was expected to win today too, but I guess someone else will get a turn now.'

'No they won't.' Callie relaxed then, looking pleased. 'It's at the ninth diamond joust that Lancelot wears the Lily Maid's favour. He wears different armour and carries a different shield — and he wins the ninth diamond for the Lily Maid.'

She shook her head as they all stared blankly at her. 'Don't you see? It means he's got to be there. And if he is, I'll find him.' She swung around and faced Lev. 'Do you know who Lavaine was?'

Lev shook his head.

'He was the Lily Maid's brother.'

'Who was the Lily Maid?'

'Elaine of Astolat. Also known as the Lady of Shalott.'

'That's where Lancelot thought we came from,' said Stephen. 'We told him Australia, but he called it Astolat.'

'And I am Elaine of Astolat, not you!' El jumped out of bed and stood beside her sister. 'I'm going to the tournament.'

'You've had your turn. It's my turn now.'

'It's not safe!'

'Then we'll swap clothes. I'll pretend to be you.' Before El could stop her, Callie snatched up the scarlet gown and pulled it over her head. 'No-one will know the difference. You can stay here in my place and — I dunno — maybe you can find a way to get us home?' She tipped some water into the bowl and hastily washed her hands and face.

'But you can't leave the tower. Remember what happened to the Lady of Shalott?' El grabbed her wrist.

'I have to take the chance, don't you see? It's my last chance to meet Lancelot.' Callie wiped her face dry on her sleeve. 'Anyway, it's my decision, not yours. But don't worry about it. No-one can make me lie down in a boat and commit suicide if I don't want to. Nothing's going to happen to me.'

'I can see why you need to go,' Meg agreed. Stephen nodded, lending his support, while Lev wondered what they were all on about now.

Looking mutinous, El sat down on the bed. Callie put on her shoes, and with a joyous sense of escape, she led the way down the stairs and out of the tower.

The sonorous notes of the church bell tolled the hour as they set off across the fields of barley and rye in the direction of the gaily coloured silken tents pitched in a meadow before them.

Callie breathed deeply, partly to make the most of the fresh air with its scent of new-mown hay and partly to still the mixture of panic and anticipation that was tying her stomach in knots.

'I'm going to prowl around and find Lancelot,' she said, as they neared the meadow.

'And I'll find Bors, see if he needs another squire,' said Stephen. He added snidely, 'I suppose you'll be leading the charge, Sir Lavaine?'

'I don't know how to ride.'

Stephen sniffed. 'That'd be right.'

'You'll have to learn.' Meg looked worried. 'They'll expect you to know how.'

'I know how to ride,' said Stephen, rubbing it in.

'Then maybe you can teach Lev?' Meg cast an anxious glance at Callie. She had hurried on ahead, impatient not to waste any more time.

'On what?'

'Maybe your friend Bors can find a spare horse?'

Stephen grunted. But he didn't dismiss the idea. It would be nice to impress Bors and Howell with his equestrian skills. After years of being packed off to various camps during school holidays, riding was something Stephen was good at. He brightened, smiling to himself. Maybe it would even be enough to earn him a knighthood?

A trumpet sounded the beginning of the tournament. The babble of conversation muted to an expectant hush as two knights on horseback faced each other across the field. Visors down and lances at the ready, they waited for the signal. Callie peered anxiously at the crowd: at the knights assembled, waiting for their turn to win glory, and the ladies sheltering from the sun under a clump of trees beside a large marquee.

One knight stood alone, his visor down so that his features were hidden. Callie sucked in her breath and her heartbeat quickened to a thunderous gallop. It was impossible to recognise him, but she knew Lancelot with a knowledge beyond sight, with a recognition that cut across time and space. This was a meeting of the spirit. With sure and steady steps, she hurried towards him.

'Lancelot!'

'Sssh!' He swung around to face her. 'My name is not known here.' The dark eyes that peered through the visor widened in shock. 'But you are not the Lady Elaine, surely? You are the fairy from the tower.' He bowed, awkward in his stiff armour, then took Callie's hand and pressed it. 'Lady Charlotte.'

A shock jolted through Callie at his touch.

'Why have you left that place?' Lancelot continued. 'Does not a spell keep you trapped there?'

'I had to see you.' A sense of urgency made Callie bold. 'I want you to wear my favour in the tourney today.' Before he had time to reject her offer, she pulled at the loose threads that kept her pearl-embroidered sleeves in place, and handed a sleeve to Lancelot.

'But I have never before worn a lady's favour.'

'Then it will add to your disguise if you do so today.'

With a smile and a murmur of thanks, he fastened the sleeve to his helmet. 'And in return you must wear this for me.' He produced the same glossy black cloak that had warmed Lev after his ducking in the river, and draped it over Callie's bare arms. He turned then to untie his horse, a large bay borrowed for the occasion, just as his unmarked armour and white shield had been borrowed.

'Don't go!' Callie clutched at his arm, feeling the chain mail rough and hard under her fingers. 'Tell me of the queen. What really happened last night?' She held her breath, dreading to hear of Lancelot's love for Guinevere.

'The queen carries no blame for Sir Patrise's death.' Lancelot's dark gaze mesmerised Callie. 'At first it was thought that he had been taken by the same mysterious disease that has killed a servant visiting the tower where you yourself reside.'

Callie thought back to the sombre funeral she had witnessed. 'What mysterious disease?'

'An affliction that spreads all over the body, with black boils and putrescence. The servant was from Maelgwyn's court at Gwynedd, come to visit his family here. 'Tis said he died in great agony, and that others now show signs of the same disease.'

'But not Sir Patrise?'

'No. He was inspected most carefully for the signs, but showed none of them.'

Callie wondered if Lancelot would tell her how he'd had to defend the Queen's honour, but instead he said, 'It seems there was a private grievance between Sir Patrise and Sir Pinel. Nimue, the Lady of the Lake, who has the Sight, informed King Arthur that it was

Pinel who poisoned the apple that killed Patrise. He has now fled the court, a true sign of his guilt. The matter is closed.'

So why have you run away, then? Callie thought she could read the answer in Lancelot's tormented expression as he gazed across the meadow in the direction of Guinevere and the ladies of the court. She had to save him from Guinevere. She had to save him from himself.

'Why do the knights not ride with stirrups?' she asked, to take his mind from the queen. It was a question that had struck her at her first sight of the jousting knights, but forgotten the moment she saw Lancelot. But she was curious to know the answer.

'Stirrups?'

Callie wondered how to explain what she meant. She untied her girdle, threw it over the bay's saddle and looped up one end of it. 'The stirrups are attached to each side of the saddle,' she said, and went on to explain how the feet slotted into the loops. 'It'll give you much more control over your horse.'

Lancelot took the girdle from Callie's hand, his chain mail brushing her dress as he leaned over the horse to study her makeshift stirrups. She took a shaky breath and closed her eyes as their bodies touched.

She felt the warmth of his breath against her cheek. 'I shall arrange for the stirrups to be crafted as you say. We shall give them a proper trial.'

Callie opened her eyes. 'It'll help you in battle as well as in tournaments.' She fought to keep her voice steady.

'Indeed.' Lancelot nodded. 'We already have the advantage over our enemies because we fight on horseback rather than on foot. It is the old Roman way, you know. But with your stirrups, we shall become invincible!'

Callie laughed at the pride in his voice.

He grasped her hand, suddenly serious. 'I would that I had met you before this day, lady.' He spoke so quietly she could hardly hear his words. 'You have put a spell of enchantment upon me. I vow I could have learned to love you more than life itself.'

'It's not too late. We can still love each other.' Callie pulled his hand against her heart, holding it tight. She couldn't fail now. She couldn't bear it if he walked away from her.

'I have pledged my loyalty and my life to the queen's service.' Lancelot released his hand and clambered awkwardly onto his horse. 'I know good fortune will ride with your favour and I thank you for it,' he said, giving her a formal salute.

In despair, Callie watched him gallop off to join the group of knights. Stephen was already there, in company with a broad-chested, barrel-shaped knight and Howell, who was almost helpless with laughter as he tried to help Lev mount a huge horse. Meg hovered uncertainly at the edge of the group. Unable to give up on Lancelot just yet, Callie walked over to her.

'This is all very blokey, isn't it?' She cast a glance at the ladies seated under the trees who were being waited on by busy cup-bearers and pages. 'Why don't we join them?'

'They might try to find out where we come from. What'll we tell them?'

'We'll think of something. I really want to meet Guinevere.' Callie felt the familiar prick of hatred as she studied the queen. Guinevere stood at the centre of the group, her status confirmed by the gold coronet circling her forehead. 'Know thine enemy.' Callie intended to make sure she did.

She dragged Meg towards the trees, and dropped a curtsey at the queen's feet.

'Lady Elaine.' The voice was cool, unfriendly. With a shock, Callie realised that of course the queen thought they had already met.

'My lady.' She wasn't quite sure how she was supposed to address Guinevere. She stood up, to find the queen staring at her with undisguised animosity. 'You are wearing Lance's cloak.' It was a statement, not a question. 'Is he here today?' Guinevere took a few steps forward, scanning the figures of the knights with unconcealed eagerness.

'He prefers to remain unknown, Ma'am.'

'And yet he has made himself known to you. I

wonder why.' Guinevere swung around to study Callie. 'So young,' she murmured. 'And so beautiful.' There was a frosty glitter of anger in her eyes. Callie knew she did not mean the words as flattery but rather as a desolate statement of fact. She looked more closely at the queen.

Despite Guinevere's beauty, the signs of age were unmistakable. Silver threaded her long golden hair and fine lines creased her pale complexion. A slight thickening at the waist added maturity to a once girlish figure. Callie fought down a sudden urge to comfort her rival.

'Nimue?' Guinevere spoke without shifting her gaze from Callie.

'What is it, Gwen?' A woman in a silvery cloak materialised at the queen's side.

'What do you see?'

Nimue's glance rested thoughtfully on Callie. Her eyes widened then, and she took a sudden breath. 'The fairy from the tower.'

'Elaine of Astolat,' Callie prompted.

'You come from another realm,' Nimue contradicted her.

'What business has she with Lance?' the queen demanded.

But Nimue pressed her lips together and would not answer. She looked downcast. Callie wondered why. Was it because, whatever happened, the legend would play itself out? Lancelot and Guinevere would be discovered; Guinevere would flee to a nunnery and Lancelot to exile, returning too late to help Arthur fight Mordred at the Battle of Camlann? Or was it because …? The thought made Callie's heart beat faster. Was it because Nimue had seen that Callie would win Lancelot, and Guinevere would lose the man she loved?

The next thought checked her excitement. If that happened, surely Camelot would be saved? Wouldn't that make the priestess happy?

'Nimue?' Guinevere pleaded.

'Remember Gwen, you cannot change what the Moirae have chosen for you.' Nimue turned away and seemed to vanish among the ladies of the court.

Callie stole a glance at Guinevere. There was a wet gleam of tears in her eyes. She blinked a couple of times and then turned a glassy stare on Callie.

'The Moirae,' she said, with a pathetic attempt at a smile. 'If we only knew what the Fates have in mind for us, perhaps we could embrace our destiny more cheerfully.' She linked an arm through Callie's and turned to the ladies in her entourage. 'This is the Lady Elaine. As Lancelot's friend, she is welcome at the court.' She beckoned Meg forward and linked arms with her too. 'The Lady Margaret,' she announced. 'Come, let us go out and greet the knights and bid them good fortune.' She set off across the meadow, towing Callie and Meg on either side of her. Callie wondered if it was merely good breeding that prompted the demonstration, or the hope that through Callie she would find Lancelot.

The king's voice rose above a cheerful hum of conversation. 'God speed, Sir Kay. But I think you should have dined less heartily last night; your horse seems heavily burdened this day.'

'I may eat for two, Your Majesty, but my horse is strong enough for both of me.' There was a shout of laughter as Sir Kay wheeled his horse around, sending him at a gallop to the lists.

Lancelot lingered at the back of the crowd. As he saw the queen approach, he bent his head and shuffled close behind two knights. Callie looked away, fixing her gaze on several other knights in turn, trying to throw the queen off the scent. She would not betray Lancelot.

The clang of steel on steel caught her attention. The two knights turned and rode full tilt towards each other once more, each trying to unseat his opponent. The noise of clashing weapons mingled with the stamp and gallop of the horses' hooves, the grunts of the combatants and the roars of approval from the onlookers. Above their heads, coloured flags flapped in the wind. The setting looked exactly like illustrations that she'd seen, yet the actions seemed futile somehow. She looked around for Stephen and Howell.

They were doing their best to shout instructions to Lev as he tried to control his horse and stay in the saddle. He didn't appear to be enjoying his riding lesson. Stirrups would have helped him too.

She moved away from Guinevere and Meg, thinking that she might go over and join them.

'Arthur!' The queen's voice stopped her. Callie bobbed a curtsey, then looked up at the king with undisguised curiosity.

'Lady Elaine. I hope you are recovered from your dunking in the river yesterday?'

'Yes, Sire. I thank you.'

'Arthur, here's a vexing situation. I do believe Lance is here today, in disguise. Perhaps you may persuade the Lady Elaine to disclose his whereabouts?'

Arthur frowned.

Wondering how Guinevere could be so thick-skinned after everything that had happened recently, Callie said quickly, 'Alas, I cannot see him, Sire.' Despite herself, her gaze raked the field. To her relief, she realised her words were true. Where was Lancelot? Where had he gone?

'Little minx!' Only Callie could guess at the desperate effort that kept the queen's tone so playful. 'I do believe she means to tease us.'

'For God's sake, Guinevere, have you no shame?' The king's lips were close to the queen's ear, but Callie heard his words clearly enough.

Guinevere's ivory skin suffused with pink. She turned away and suddenly became very interested in the activities of the knights on the field.

'I am sure Lancelot has his reasons for keeping away,' King Arthur said more loudly. 'Meanwhile I must talk to Kay about the presentation of the ninth diamond, and the celebration to follow.'

'Stay with me!' The queen swivelled and clutched his arm, but he shook her off and hurried away, clapping several knights on the shoulder as he passed, and pausing to swap banter with three others. The queen stood silent with bent head and drooping shoulders, defeat written in the lines of her graceful body. Was this the pattern of their lives together? Or was Arthur punishing her for his humiliation at court?

Guinevere made no further effort to trap Callie into betraying Lancelot's whereabouts. Leaning heavily on Nimue's arm, she allowed the Lady of the Lake to lead her back to a seat underneath the trees. Callie watched her go, as pity and a wild, triumphant joy waged war in her heart.

Her skin prickled and she turned. Lancelot. It was almost as if she was joined to him. She could sense him before she even saw him. His hand touched her back. She felt her body heat under his fingertips. He gazed down at her with burning dark eyes. 'Lady,' he said on a low breath.

'Take care, Lancelot. The queen knows you are here but not who you are,' Callie said quickly.

He nodded. 'If I win today, the ninth diamond is yours.' Without waiting for her reply, he dug his heels into the horse's side and trotted away.

Callie clasped her hands together, at once afraid yet jubilant. Lancelot was drawn to her, just as she was to him. Which meant that she, Callie, had the power to undo whatever misguided loyalty kept him at the queen's side. It was only a matter of time, unless El succeeded in zapping them back, which seemed highly unlikely. Whatever the cost, she would continue her quest.

'You've got to help me,' El demanded.

At the sound of the unknown voice, the young servant girl jerked back in alarm, pushing her hands to her face. She had been brushing splatters of fat and ashes from what looked like a huge open fireplace, although a greasy spit across the enclave told its true purpose. Her hands and feet were charcoal black and filthy, and there were black smudges across her cheeks. She lowered her hands and stared at El as if she'd seen a ghost.

Hard-eyed, fighting panic, El stared back at her. Panic, and a growing sense of impotent frustration had driven her out of the tower room and down the stairs in search of someone, anyone, for company and for help. For hours she had paced the room, wondering how Callie had survived their absence for all that time. She knew now how hard it was to be alone and afraid, in a place she didn't know and most desperately wanted to leave. The dead rat hadn't helped. Once the others had left, she'd noticed a curious smell in the room. Of death. Decay. Taking small, reluctant breaths, she had tracked down its source.

Shuddering, she'd pulled the body up by its tail and tossed it out the window. Abandoning the notion of painting anything, she had started pacing around the room, side-stepping the furniture. For variety then, she had turned and paced in the other direction. Until she realised that if she stayed any longer, she would go insane. So she'd wrenched open the door and fled downstairs.

The young girl wiped her hands down the sides of her smock and bobbed a shy curtsey. 'Madam,' she whispered, keeping her head bent so she wouldn't have to confront the stranger.

Apart from the young servant and El, the kitchen was empty. The cluttered table spoke of a hasty exit: a flap of pastry and a rolling pin; a basket of eggs; a scatter of aromatic plants, violets, parsley, primroses. A half-plucked goose lay at the end of the table, its long neck and head drooping off the edge. Fire blazed in a huge hearth, twin to the one being cleaned out by the girl. Above the fire hung a cooking pot, from which emanated a rich scent of beef stew. The carcass of a pig was skewed on a spit at the front of the fire. The young girl followed El's glance and hastily cranked the spit handle around. Drips of meat juice and fat splattered and flared. Flaming torches added their smoky breath to the smell of cooking.

'Where is everyone?'

The girl poked a thumb over her shoulder, towards one of the stone arches leading from the kitchen. El became aware of a heated conversation taking place in the alcove beyond, amid the clink and clatter of dishes.

Not sure what she was hoping for, she walked to the opening. Silence fell as the occupants of the room stopped arguing and turned to stare. El glanced around the group, her curiosity caught by a shadowy figure dressed in black standing beside a pillar right at the back. The woman had a pale face and dark eyes which burned with unexpected malevolence as she met El's gaze. The others seemed unaware of her presence. All their attention was focused on El. Then an elderly woman, short and plump with grey wisps of hair escaping from her bonnet, bustled forward. She grabbed the young girl and thrust her out of sight behind her ample frame.

'Is there something you want, miss?' Her lips folded down, tucked around her toothless gums. She wiped her hands down her smock, adding a patch of wet to the stain of blood and feathers.

'You've got to help me.' El hesitated. Could the woman be trusted with the truth?

She beckoned her through the arch and sat down on a bench beside the food-littered table. She wasn't sure what she was expecting as she told an edited version of their story: probably that the woman would tell her to put her faith in God, or something.

Instead, she shuffled closer and whispered hoarsely, 'The old gods may send you back to where you came from — if they have a mind to do so. A sacrifice will encourage their good favour.'

'I'll try anything, if you'll only tell me what to do.'

The woman shifted her weight from one foot to another. She didn't reply, but her red-rimmed eyes studied the rings on El's fingers and the rich ruby and pearl necklace at her throat. She blinked, then stared some more.

'I'll give you this,' El touched one of the rings, 'if you'll only help me?'

The woman licked her lips, but remained silent.

'This?' El touched the necklace. The woman nodded. Fumbling slightly with the unfamiliar clasp, El undid the necklace and held it out. It vanished instantly up a capacious sleeve. She wondered if she'd been conned, but the woman leaned forward. 'You must call the Earth Mother from her *sid*, from her home under the hill,' she said, and went on then to describe the rest of the rite.

El listened, desperately trying to remember the whispered instructions. She wished she had a pad and pencil to make notes.

'There are five of us here,' she said, as the woman finished her recital. 'Will the old gods help all of us?'

The woman nodded.

'Will you come up and show me what to do?'

'No!' She held up two fingers in a sign against evil. ''Tis said upstairs is bewitched by the High Priestess, Morgan. Some say she is a sorceress. None will interfere with her magic.'

'Then how do I know if your spell will work?' El fought down a sudden urge to laugh. Spells? Witchcraft? She must be going crazy!

The woman regarded her with a serious expression. 'You cannot know if the Goddess will help you,' she said. 'But if you would rather seek the help of the High Priestess?'

For a moment, El was tempted. To meet the celebrated Morgan le Fay, to dabble in black magic …

'No, I'll try your spell first.' Her lips moved as she rehearsed the instructions she'd been given.

'I will gather what you need. Wait here.' The old

woman hurried through the arch, drawing the young girl after her, away from harm.

As El waited for her to return, she idly scratched her arm. It felt itchy. She shuddered. Perhaps it was a flea from the dead rat. Please let us get home, she thought. I can't stand it here. Please let me be able to do what Callie can't.

'So what's the story with Lancelot, then?' Meg asked as she and Callie stood in the hot, dusty evening, watching the last of the jousts. Two by two, the knights had engaged in combat through the afternoon, thrusting at each other with their lances, each trying to be the first to unseat his opponent.

The last two knights broke, wheeled, then charged again, galloping towards each other, shields on guard and lances at the ready. More clashes and buffeting. It had been the same all day. It had become boring after the first few rounds, although Callie had felt her stomach tighten in fear and anticipation each time Lancelot had taken to the field. He'd fought well, excelled at everything.

Except this time. As she watched, she heard Lancelot's opponent yell a warning as their lances clashed. Quick as a flash, he pulled out a short sword and turned on Lancelot, the last rays of the sun tinting the polished blade blood red. There was a gasp from the crowd as the blade missed Lancelot's shield and pierced his side. He jerked, then slumped forward.

Callie started to run, but before she had taken many steps, Lancelot heaved himself upright. His fingers closed over the weapon. He gave a sharp tug, then threw the bloody sword at his opponent, who tried to catch it and missed. Lancelot noticed Callie then, and held up his arm, commanding her to stay back in the crowd.

A third knight galloped onto the field and set his horse between the two, urging them both to withdraw. Callie recognised Stephen's friend as Lancelot's opponent when Bors pulled down his visor and cried, 'I'll know you yet!' It was clear he had no intention of giving up the quest.

But the third knight shouted, 'King's orders! There will be no bloodshed today.' He caught the reins of the horse and dragged Bors away.

Hunched forward in the saddle and obviously in pain, Lancelot rode from the field into the dense shadows of the forest beyond. Callie wondered if she should have told him that, despite this setback, he would win the ninth diamond? Perhaps he might have stayed then?

'That was Lancelot, wasn't it?' Meg came to stand beside Callie.

Despairing, Callie nodded. She shivered, and hugged Lancelot's cloak more closely around her shoulders.

'I recognised your sleeve.' Meg nudged her friend. 'Cheer up. He'll be back to pick up his reward.'

'I hope so.' If he did she would be there, the first to congratulate him, and to kiss him if she dared.

She turned and noticed Stephen slowly ambling in their direction, closely followed by Howell who was leading Lev on a horse. 'Stephen looks different somehow,' she commented.

'Yeah. He's happy,' said Meg.

Startled, Callie looked more closely. It was true. Stephen was smiling as he threw a comment over his shoulder. Howell jabbed the air with his fist. Stephen pretended to duck and they both laughed.

'He's found a friend,' Meg added.

Callie thought back to the lonely, boastful boy on the bus. 'Yeah, you're right. I'm glad he's happy here.'

'You talking about me again?' Stephen stepped up to them.

'We never stop.'

Stephen laughed as he reached in front of Howell and grabbed the reins, jerking the horse to a standstill. 'Get off!' he told Lev. Startled by the sudden action, the horse reared. Howell moved forward to gentle it, making soft chucking noises. Lev clung to its mane and looked frightened.

'Everyone's going to the pavilion,' Meg said. 'Maybe they're going to hand out the prize.'

Howell helped Lev to dismount. They moved to join the crowd gathering inside the large tent with its bright, multicoloured bunting, leaving Howell to tether the horse to a nearby tree.

'Well met!' The knight who had fought Lancelot hurried over to them. Callie bit her lip, struggling against the urge to tell him off.

'This is Bors,' Meg introduced Callie.

'Lady Elaine.' Bors looked slightly bewildered at being introduced to someone he'd already met.

Callie tried to collect her drifting thoughts. 'Thank you for the loan of a horse,' she said with a sidelong glance at Lev who scowled as he rubbed his sore backside.

Bors grinned at Lev. 'I do not think you enjoyed the experience?'

'Nuh.' And then, as Lev felt Callie's foot connect with his shin, 'But I'll learn.'

'To the unknown knight goes the honour of the day.' King Arthur's voice boomed out across the high-pitched chatter of the ladies and the lower voices of their escorts. For once he and the queen were together, seated side-by-side on huge, ornately carved chairs. A sudden hush was followed by a wild burst of applause as Lancelot stepped forward. Callie waited for him to raise his visor and reveal himself. But he did not. Instead, he kneeled before the king to accept the diamond.

'Our congratulations, Sire. You fought bravely and with honour through the day. All victories were yours, save the last.' King Arthur flicked a reproachful glance at Sir Bors, who shuffled his feet and muttered something under his breath.

Guinevere leaned closer, her glance shifting from the red sleeve on the knight's helmet to Callie and back again. Her face turned pale. She peered through the visor, seeking the man inside. Knowing that Lancelot had been recognised, Callie waited for him to present the diamond to the queen. But he did not. Instead, he bowed to them all, then slipped quietly out of the tent. Guinevere clasped her hand to her breast. She looked wretched. But she did not betray him.

'I am sure I know that knight. He seems familiar somehow,' Bors commented, as the crowd filtered slowly out of the tent after Lancelot.

'Why did you try to kill him?' Meg queried.

'I did not!' Bors sounded shocked. 'I asked him to reveal his true identity, but he refused. I was curious. I thought the point of the sword might persuade him to make himself known. I had no intention of wounding him but my horse surged forward before I had a chance to set my sword aside.'

Should she reveal Lancelot's secret? Before she could decide, Callie noticed him standing in the shadows of a clump of trees. He was alone. She could not waste this opportunity. She walked across to him, her path silvered by the light of the moon which shone also on her, changing her to a faerie creature of moonlight and shadow. As she came to Lancelot's side, he unfastened the scarlet sleeve from his helmet and presented it to her. 'As I foretold, lady, your favour brought me good fortune today.'

'It was your skill that won the prize.' Callie took the sleeve, watching with eager eyes as Lancelot unclipped his visor and pushed it up.

For the first time she saw his face up close. It was shadowed black and white by the moonlight. He seemed unfamiliar, almost a phantom. Dark lines furrowed his forehead and bracketed his mouth. He was much older than she had imagined, but he carried himself with strength and assurance. Unable to stop herself, she reached out to him and gently traced the frosting of grey among the black lock of hair falling onto his forehead.

'Lady Charlotte.' His voice was husky as he caught her hand and kissed it. Unaware that they were watched, unable to bear it any longer, Callie threw her arms around his neck and kissed him, feeling a liquid golden sweetness flood her body as his lips met hers. This, then, was what it was all about. This was why she was here. Lancelot was her destiny. By making him love her she could save the court of Camelot from destruction. A wild thrumming happiness filled her as his arms tightened around her, as she sensed his desperate need. Then he thrust her from him, his breathing ragged as he struggled for control.

''Tis not seemly …'

'I don't care,' Callie whispered. 'I've come such a long way to find you, to be with you.' She looked up at him and saw the desire, and fear, in his eyes. She clutched his hand tightly, an anchor in a spinning world, and willed him to speak of love.

'Guinevere!' He snatched his hand away.

She followed the direction of his glance, and snapped stiff with shock as she saw the queen standing just a few paces away, staring at them.

Lancelot bowed. Hastily, Callie curtsied.

The queen's expression spoke of hatred and loss. But she said only, 'You fought well today, Lance. You deserved to win. I trust Bors did you no great harm?'

'Just a scratch, m'lady.' Lancelot's formal tone matched the queen's.

She hesitated, then turned on her heel and left them, not speaking of what was on all their minds. But she had achieved her desire. The spell was broken. Bitterly but silently, Callie cursed her.

'This is for you.' Lancelot's voice broke into her angry frustration.

Callie looked down at the hand he held out to her;

at the diamond winking in his palm, its facets reflecting the cold brilliance of moonlight.

'In return for the honour of your favour,' Lancelot explained further, as she made no move to take it.

'It's beautiful.' Callie gently touched the shining stone. 'But how can I take it from you?'

'I won it for you, just as I promised,' he reminded her.

'I shall treasure it always,' she said. With a sudden jolt of fear, she wondered just how long that would be.

Lancelot smiled. ''Tis but a cold stone, a poor thing beside the treasure that stands before me.' He bowed, then gave a low grunt of pain. He pressed his hand to his left side.

'You're hurt!' In the excitement of meeting Lancelot, Callie had forgotten how badly wounded he'd been.

''Tis nothing.' But Callie saw blood seeping between his fingers. She pulled his hand away. There was a glint of metal in the blood. The sword's sharp point must have broken off as it tore the links of chain mail.

'We must get you to a hospital.'

Lancelot blinked, puzzled, while Callie remembered where she was. What to do? She couldn't leave Lancelot like this. The wound would fester, turn septic. He could die from it.

'I'll take you to the tower,' she decided, thinking of El and her first aid certificate. 'Are you able to ride?'

Lancelot nodded. His face was white and sheened with sweat. 'If you would help me mount?'

Callie led the huge bay to a wooden stile. She helped Lancelot climb up and ease himself into the saddle. 'My sister will tend to your wounds,' she promised, trying to summon a confidence she didn't feel. 'She'll know what to do.'

She waved at the small group waiting at a tactful distance. 'We're coming with you,' she called. Together, with Stephen leading the horse Bors had given to Lev, they set off for the tower.

CHAPTER TEN

E l watched the shadows creep across the tower room as the sun sank below the horizon. She moved the fat, lighted candle she had brought from the kitchen into the centre of the room, blessing the pale circle of light that helped to hold back the darkness. She had to wait for the moon to rise, and although each minute felt like an hour, she was less frightened now that she had a plan, something to do, something she hoped with all her heart would get them out of Camelot and back home.

She allowed herself a small grin at her own expense. How she'd laughed — jeered — at Meg and her incantations. Just as well Meg wasn't here to witness what she was going to do now.

Once more she rehearsed the instructions and the chant that she had devised, memorising them so that she would not fail. She could not fail. She couldn't bear to think they might be stuck here forever. What would Dad think if they just disappeared? And Gran? What about Greg? El tried to take comfort from the thought of him, but the question nagged her: How long would it take him to find someone else to go out with if they never came back? Not long, probably. Girls were always trying it on with Greg, but so far he'd shown no interest. El closed her eyes and summoned up his image: tall, muscular, tanned. So twenty-first century compared with the guys around Camelot.

But they were at Camelot and Greg wasn't. She wished with all her heart that she'd made Callie put him in. Then he'd be here with her now, sharing this horrible experience. What was he doing, back in Sydney? Was he worried? Was he missing her?

Her arm itched, and she scratched it. It was already sore from her scratching, but the more she scratched, the more it itched, until it seemed as if her whole body was on fire. She straightened her arms, held them rigid by her side, and felt her skin throb with her need.

A flash of red caught her eye. Callie? She walked across to the mirror and peered closer, not quite brave enough to go to the window. She couldn't risk activating the legend again. Not if it meant Callie's death.

A red cloak. A group of young women on their way home from the market. A burst of laughter. They were being teased by two village lads. Too tired to talk, a couple of farm labourers trudged home behind them, their scythes balanced across their shoulders, the metal gleaming dark in the fading light.

El raised her hand to her neck, touching skin instead of the heavy ruby and pearl necklace. She wished the old woman well of her bargain, but wondered if the necklace was worth anything. The old woman would be angry if it turned out to be a fake. But they wouldn't be around to bear her anger, so it didn't matter. If we don't go anywhere it means the old woman failed me, just as I failed her, El thought.

The moon eased above the horizon; a glowing orb in the dark, star-spattered sky. In two days it would be a complete circle. The old woman had warned her to act tonight, to make the most of the moon's power. But El had no intention of delaying anyway. It was time now to start the preparations.

She picked up the pitcher and poured some water into the basin. Then she stripped off the long dress and shift underneath and carefully washed herself.

Purification.

She dressed once more, and now she had to face the part of the ceremony she was most dreading. Sacrifice.

El shuddered. She crumbled up some of the mouldy cheese she'd begged from the old woman and spread the pieces over the floor. Then she picked up a sharp knife and stood back, quiet and still. Waiting. Watching.

The biggest rat came first. The leader of the pack. Eyes bright, whiskers quivering, he dived onto a piece of cheese and set about devouring it. With squeaks of anticipation, their claws clicking on the stone flagging, the rest of them swarmed out until the floor became a heaving carpet of brown fur.

El watched them, fighting hysteria and the need to escape. *This is our last chance to get home.* The thought pulsed through her brain, almost drowned by the scream rising at the back of her throat. In an effort to calm herself, she said the words out loud. 'This is our last chance to get home.' Then she began to repeat them again and again, like a mantra, as she raised the knife and stepped towards the wriggling bodies. The rats ignored her, too intent on their feast to care; perhaps too unused to human company to fear the danger.

'This is our last chance to get home.' El plunged the knife down, taking the rat's head from its body in one wild stroke. Blood spurted over the stone floor, spattering splashes of ruby on the green fabric of her dress. With panic-stricken cries, the rats scrambled over and around one another, desperate to reach their boltholes. Within seconds the room was cleared. Except for the body of the headless rat.

'A sacrifice,' the old woman had said. 'To win the favour of the Old Gods.'

El looked down at the dead rat with disgust. This was the best she could manage.

She picked up the carcass and threw it out the window. Carefully, she placed the head in the centre of the room. She looked around then for Callie's box of paints and paintbrush. With frequent trips to the basin of water to moisten the brush, she painted a large circle around the rat's head with a square inside, its four corners touching the wavering line of the circle.

Earth, air, fire, water. She placed a bowl of sand at one corner and tipped water from the pitcher into another bowl, which she placed opposite. Carefully, she settled the fat tallow candle at the third corner. The corner nearest the window she left empty, hoping that the cool air wafting through would be enough to signify her intention. Now what?

The tapers for the circle of light. She removed some from the bundle she'd brought up with her and lit each one in turn, placing them around the circle she had painted on the stone flagging. The flames sputtered then steadied, shedding a radiant glow in the dark shadowy room. Briefly, El took time to acknowledge how bad it must have been for Callie here alone in the dark for all those hours with only the rats for company. Her twin was much braver than she'd imagined.

But I'm still the one who has to bail us out of trouble and get us back. There was satisfaction in the thought.

She stepped into the square within the circle of light. 'Great Mother,' she whispered, 'Queen of Heaven. Grant me your presence here tonight.'

She felt in the purse at her waist for the herbs the old woman had given her, and scattered them about the circle. Celandine, laurel, furze, mint and vervain. Some of them caught the flames from the candles, giving off a pungent fragrance as they sizzled.

'Turn widdershins twice, then twice in the opposite direction,' the old woman had instructed. Slowly, El turned anticlockwise. The scent from the herbs was making her feel light-headed. She circled the other way, then fell to her knees and closed her eyes. Her hands folded naturally in prayer. She began the chant she had spent the afternoon and evening composing:

'Goddess of going, heed our plight,
Make our journey safe tonight;
Take us over land and foam
To the place that we call home.

Help us travel time and space
To loving families in an unknown place.
Mother Goddess, heed our plight
Take us safely home tonight.'

El stayed kneeling, her hands folded, waiting for something to happen. But she heard only silence, as still as the grave.

It was broken by a soft thumping. Footsteps, sounding louder now, coming closer. Before she had time to move, the door flung open.

'What on earth are you doing?' Meg stopped dead in amazement. 'Whew, it pongs in here!' she added, glancing at the lighted tapers and smoking herbs.

The others crowded around, peering over her shoulder to see what was going on.

'Invoking the help of the Mother Goddess to take us home.' El scrambled to her feet as Lancelot hastily crossed himself.

'Yuk! What's that?' Meg broke the circle of light as she stepped forward and picked up the rat's bloody head. 'El, how could you?' She threw it out the window before El could stop her.

'The old ways.' Lancelot crossed himself once more. 'You would do better to put your faith in Christ, lady.'

'We already tried that,' El retorted.

'Prayers to the Goddess?' Meg giggled. 'Oh El, you don't believe in that high magic stuff, surely?'

'It's no different from the white magic you believe in,' El retaliated. 'Anyway, I had to try something to get us back.'

'Well, we're still here.' Meg couldn't resist it.

'I bet you're the only one who wants to get back,' Callie told her sister, with a quick glance at the others for reassurance.

'I want to leave too,' Meg said loyally, pulling El out of the circle of light. 'Can I get rid of this now?' Without waiting for an answer, she emptied the contents of the bowls out the window, then picked up the tapers. She dribbled some wax from them onto the top of the cupboard and clumped them together in the hot liquid, holding them until they were set firm. 'Now we can see,' she said.

'El! You have to take care of Lancelot.' Callie's thoughts were never far from the knight who had come to fill her heart and mind. 'He was hurt at the tournament. A sword wound. Look!'

El hurried to Lancelot to inspect the rusty red patch seeping through the torn metal links of his armour.

'Can you help him? I think part of Bors' sword is still stuck in his side.'

El swallowed hard. She parted the cut in Lancelot's hauberk. Her face paled as she took in the full extent of the wound.

'Please,' Callie pleaded. 'You're the only one who knows what to do.'

El straightened her shoulders. 'Go down to the kitchen and get a pot of boiling water,' she commanded Meg. 'Explain what's happened, and ask if they've got any sort of herbs or poultices for wounds. There's a fat, toothless old woman down there. If you give her some of your jewellery, she'll give you whatever you ask for.'

'I'll help you.' Stephen followed Meg out of the room, leaving El still fussing. 'I wish we had some antibiotics. And he could probably do with a tetanus injection as well.' As she spoke, she'd been busy clearing the table. Now she gestured at Lancelot. 'Take off your armour and lie down.'

'But …' His hands folded across his chest in a protective gesture.

'I have to see what I'm doing.' El tugged at the rough chain mail tunic, trying to pull it over his head.

Lancelot winced. El looked down, and felt immediately faint and sick as the bleeding wound was exposed. She sucked in a quick breath, and tugged harder. Callie came up beside her and gripped Lancelot's hand. He held on to her like a drowning man.

'I'll help you.' Reluctantly, Lev stepped forward and helped to ease the hauberk over Lancelot's head. He set it on a bench and sat down beside it.

For the first time, Lev felt clear-headed and fresh. From time to time, pains still cramped his legs and belly, but they were bearable now, and easing all the time. But thanks to El's brutal honesty, he no longer felt good about himself, about who he was inside. Everyone thought he was a hero but really he was just a street kid who lived on his wits, cheating people and stealing whatever came his way. He wasn't proud of the way he lived. He just didn't know how else to survive.

Lancelot groaned with pain.

'Lie still,' El commanded, as he tried to move away from her probing fingers. 'Got it!' She eased the metal tip out of his side and raised a face shiny with triumph. Lev wanted to hit her. It was El's fault he felt the way he did. The rest of them were having a great time, making the most of Camelot. They didn't have to pretend to be something they weren't. They could fit in without any problem. Not like him. The outcast. The misfit. The good for nothing. Hell, he couldn't even ride. His bum really hurt. He shifted on the hard bench, trying to ease the soreness. And it was all for nothing. They'd take his knighthood away, just as soon as they found out the truth. He glared at El. Why couldn't she have kept her mouth shut and let him believe that he was someone special? Better to face the truth than live a lie? Lev rubbed his face in despair.

Lancelot moaned softly. His face was white and wet with sweat. He looked on the verge of passing out. Callie gripped his hand tighter. 'It's all right,' she whispered. 'El knows what she's doing. She'll fix you up.'

'The wound needs to be stitched, really. I'll just have to bind it as tightly as I can.' El stepped over to the linen sheet that had formed Callie's canvas and tore off several long strips.

'Here's the boiling water.' Meg held the door and stepped aside as Stephen staggered in behind her with a large cauldron. 'And here's a paste of crushed woundwort leaves, and some syrup for the pain.' She set down a shallow dish containing a stinking green paste and a cup of liquid.

Lev leaned forward and took a hopeful sniff. Poppy syrup! He lunged forward to grab the cup but Callie knocked his hand away. With a reproachful glance, she raised Lancelot's head and helped him drink the potion, while El dipped a strip of linen into the boiling water and set about cleaning Lancelot's wound.

'So what was that dead rat all about?' Meg asked.

'A sacrifice to the Mother Goddess,' El replied, adding briskly to mask her disappointment, 'It doesn't seem to have worked, though. Did you see that old woman down in the kitchen? She's the one who told me what to do. She gave me all the stuff I had to use.'

'Yes, we saw her.' Meg frowned. 'She's wearing your necklace and acting like the Queen of Sheba. But they're worried about something down there. They were having a council of war when we walked in. And they didn't want to know about us. They seemed to be blaming the old woman for their problems. I had to hand over all my jewellery before she'd help us.' Meg touched her bare neck. 'She's going to spew when she finds out it's all as worthless as the spell she gave you.'

Eyes closed and gritting his teeth against the pain of El's administrations, Lancelot mumbled, 'Morgan le Fay.'

'Who?' Meg bent closer to hear his voice. Lancelot didn't reply.

'You mean the old woman in the kitchen?'

'Mayhaps it is Morgan. She is a shape-shifter. She takes many forms. She has magical powers. Evil powers that cause harm.'

'Like wanting Mordred to be king instead of Arthur?'

Lancelot's eyes flicked open. 'Is that his ambition?' He struggled to sit up, but El pushed him down again.

'No! Not really.' Meg tried to undo the harm she might have caused by her careless words. 'He told me last night at the feast that his mother, Morgause, and his aunt Morgan le Fay have high hopes for him, but that he himself has only loyalty and love for Arthur.' She didn't dare confess what she'd read in Mordred's eyes when he'd looked at the queen.

'The Orkney brothers.' Lancelot's voice was low and bitter with hatred. 'Did Mordred tell you that his brother Agravaine plots against me; that he tries to link my name with that of the queen and so shame us both in the eyes of the court and King Arthur? And did he tell you of his brother Gaheris, who in a fit of jealous rage murdered their own mother?'

'Never mind all that now. I'll just put some of this green stuff on to help the wound heal, and then I'll bandage you up,' said El, too intent on her job to concern herself with the intrigues of the court. She began to apply the paste, hoping the old woman knew what she was about.

As the cool green mixture soothed the wound, Lancelot's grip loosened on Callie's hand and he breathed a long sigh.

'My lord, will you leave the court and come away with me?' Callie had no intention of embarrassing Lancelot, but was thoroughly alarmed by the inform-ation she'd just heard. She had to get Lancelot away before Mordred's jealousy and ambition divided the court and set the scene for the last tragedy of Camelot.

'Lady?' Lancelot jerked upright in surprise. 'It would not be seemly —'

'Lie down!' El commanded, alarmed and furious with Callie. It wasn't because she was jealous, she reassured herself. After all, she was in love with Greg. She'd been going out with him forever. He was the first guy she'd ever really cared about.

No, her concern was all for Callie. Callie, who'd never

shown any interest in a guy before. Callie, who had always let El pull her into line, but who seemed to have found a mind of her own since they'd come to Camelot. Surely Callie knew she was wasting her time? How could she make such a fool of herself in front of everyone?

'I don't mean I want to live as your mistress,' Callie gabbled, scarlet with embarrassment. 'I'm asking you to marry me.'

'Callie! Stop it!' El pushed her sister out of the way and began to strap Lancelot's side tightly with the linen bandages.

But a sense of urgency drove Callie on. 'Even if you don't love me now, Lancelot, maybe you will in time? And I'll be a good wife to you, I promise. If we marry, Agravaine can't harm you. The king and queen will stay happily married and, with your help, King Arthur can overcome any harm that threatens him from Mordred — or from anyone else,' she added hastily as Meg gave her a sharp jab in the ribs.

'I have pledged my love and loyalty to the queen.' Lancelot sounded desolate. 'I have given my oath never to marry.'

Callie took a deep breath. 'Then I will live with you as your mistress.'

'Callie, how can you? You can't!' El stuttered into the horrified silence of the room.

'Jesu, defend me.' Lancelot crossed himself. 'I cannot permit that, for then I return your sisters and brothers much evil for their goodness.' He took Callie's hand and drew her close to him. 'For your kindness, I shall show you my care. Set your heart on a good knight who will wed you, and I shall provide you with all that you may want thereafter.'

'I only want you.' Stricken, Callie stepped away from him and turned to the window. She could not let him see her cry.

'Don't look out!' El shrieked. She sprang towards Callie to drag her away.

But Callie had looked, and seen. She had seen that they were doomed, because her quest had failed. Lancelot belonged to the queen. Nothing she could do would change that now.

'There's another funeral passing by.' She wiped her eyes on the sleeve of her gown. Her voice was thick, choked with tears as she added, 'The cart is leaving the tower. Some of the servants are going with the corpse to keep it company.'

'Let me see.' El stood beside Callie and draped an arm over her sister's shoulders, giving her a quick hug as they watched the entourage set off, accompanied by the mournful beat of a single drum. Callie leaned in to El, grateful for her comfort.

'That's the second funeral I've seen. Is it from the

same strange disease that's going around Camelot?' She kept her back turned on Lancelot.

'Not Camelot. Gwynedd. But now the sickness has come here, to the tower.' Sir Lancelot stood up from the table and, hand pressed to his side, walked over to the window and looked out over their shoulders. 'I have heard talk that its cause is the conjunction of the planets Saturn, Jupiter and Mars. But others believe it is Christ's punishment for those who still follow the old ways and that the stigmata of their shame is there for all to see.'

'What stigmata?' El's curiosity was roused at the notion of an archaic superstition that she might be able to name and even deal with.

'Black swellings. They start under the armpits, then the whole body turns black. The victims spit blood, and in three days they die.'

'The Black Death.' El whirled to face him with wide and frightened eyes. 'Bubonic plague? It's come here, to the tower?'

'I do not understand you.'

'It's a terrible disease, spread by rats. In fact, plagues have been recorded since Roman times,' El explained. 'The worst outbreak was in the fourteenth century, when it killed hundreds of thousands of people and wiped out whole villages. I remember hearing about it in the first aid class, when they told us about the wonders of antibiotics.'

'Which we don't have back in this century.' A stricken silence followed Callie's observation.

'What is this disease you speak of?' By now, Lancelot shared their concern.

'Plague is carried by the fleas that live on the bodies of diseased rats.' A shudder shook El as she remembered the dead rat she'd uncovered. Had it died of natural causes? The tower was full of them, and she'd already been bitten by their fleas. Her hand went up to scratch her arm. With an effort of will, she gripped her hands together and struggled for control.

'What's the matter?' Callie had felt her sister's fear.

El shook her head and turned to Lancelot. 'Every rat must be hunted and exterminated,' she said. 'If the plague spreads through Camelot, everyone will die — the king and queen, the knights and their ladies, the servants. Everyone.'

'No!'

'Yes. Killing the rats and their fleas is the only way to stop the plague from spreading.'

'It's a bit late. People are already dying.' Lev took a grim satisfaction in contradicting El.

'Of course it's not too late,' she said briskly, trying to ignore the itch that burned for attention. She mustn't alarm them; not yet anyway. She turned to Lancelot. 'It's only in the tower? No-one in the castle or the town shows signs of this disease?'

'No. Sir Patrise died yesterday, but he was poisoned.

I have heard only of servants living here who have died of this other thing.'

'Then you may be lucky. We may be able to isolate the plague.' El thought through the options. 'You must put a ring of fire around the walls of Camelot to keep it safe, to keep out any diseased rats. Give orders that every single rat inside the walls must be hunted out and burned,' she told Lancelot. 'And you must hurry. That funeral procession we saw is carrying the disease. You have to stop it from going any further.'

'It travels slowly,' Meg said in encouragement. 'You've got time to catch it if you hurry.'

'Do not go near it,' El said quickly. 'Call to them to bury their dead and tell them to go to the river afterwards, to wash themselves and their clothes to drown the fleas.'

'No! You can't go back to Camelot. It's not safe.' Callie whirled to confront Lancelot.

'He'll be safer in the castle than here,' El said bluntly. 'This place is full of rats.' She hesitated. Should she share her news? Yes, if it meant saving Lancelot and everyone in Camelot.

'I found a dead rat up here just this morning. I threw it out. That was before I cut off the head of that other one you saw.' Unable to bear the itching any longer, she scratched herself through the fabric of her dress.

Without saying anything, Meg grabbed El's arm and pushed up her sleeve. In silence, they all stared at the pink rash, at the small red dots of fleabites. Overcome with horror and fear, Callie began to cry.

'I've put us all in danger,' she sobbed. 'El's sick and now it's too late to save Camelot. Don't you see? That's why it was destroyed. It was nothing to do with Mordred. It was the Black Death that finished Arthur's reign.'

'Nonsense,' El said brusquely, pushing down her sleeve to hide her arm. She turned to Lancelot. 'Get out of here, quickly. Warn the funeral procession, then go to the river and wash yourself and your clothes and armour, just in case you've picked up any fleas. Then hurry to the castle and warn the king to do as I have said. Put a ring of fire around the town walls to keep Camelot safe.'

Lancelot nodded. 'I shall do as you say. But what of you, lady? Who shall care for you if you are sick?'

'Don't worry about me.' El gave him a push towards the door.

Lancelot stood his ground. 'I will go. But so must you. I cannot leave any of you here, if what you say is true. Your lives are at far greater risk than mine.'

'It's too late for us,' said El. 'For me, anyway. But you others can go if you want.' She stared at them defiantly.

'I'm not leaving you.' Callie linked arms with her sister. But she felt as if she was being ripped in half.

'Maybe you've just got a rash?' Meg suggested hopefully.

El shook her head.

'How do you feel?'

'Itchy. And I've got a bit of a headache. But that's all.'

'I have to try and get us back home. It's our only hope. Otherwise El …' But Callie couldn't bear to put her fear into words. She looked at Lancelot and struggled for control. It was much more important now to save her sister's life than to try to change a legend. But how were they to get back home? And how was she to say goodbye to Lancelot?

'Come with us!' she said urgently, clutching his arm. 'Maybe you can come with us to the twenty-first century?'

'Lady.' He took her hand, clasping it between his own. 'My duty lies here. I must go to Camelot. I must warn the king and queen of the terrible danger that lies in wait for us. But I beg you to come with me. I do not know what journey you contemplate, but you will all find shelter with us if you so desire.'

'No. I can't risk bringing the disease to court. You are safer without us.'

Not sure if Lancelot understood her, El spelled it out. 'You should have no contact with anyone who has it, or you too may sicken and die.' On impulse, she picked up a hunk of mouldy cheese and held it out; it was part of the stash she had brought from the kitchen to tempt the rats. 'You've already had contact with me, so if you should get the plague, please eat this, as much of it as you can. It might help.'

'Mouldy cheese? Yuk!' Stephen scoffed.

'Blue mould. They talked about it in the first aid class. It's how Alexander Fleming first discovered penicillin. Anyway,' she added huffily, 'it's better than nothing.'

Lancelot took the hunk of cheese and sniffed it. 'It is customary in our court to treat skin diseases by placing a dried toad on the afflicted part to draw the poison.'

'That sounds like Morgan's witchcraft. Mouldy cheese is much better.'

Lancelot nodded. He picked up the bloodstained hauberk and put it on, easing it cautiously over his bandaged wound. Callie took off the black cloak and held it out to him. He draped it over his shoulders. 'I will take my leave.' He bowed to El. 'My gratitude for treating my wound, lady. And I shall make sure that your instructions are carried out.' He bowed to the others. 'Will you not change your minds? Will you not come with me?'

'We can't.' Meg answered for them all. Callie kept silent, not trusting herself to speak or move less she embarrass herself by throwing herself at Lancelot and refusing to let go. Her eyes and throat ached with unshed tears. She felt faint with longing and grief. She would never see him again, she was sure of it.

She looked up at him as he put his arms around her.

He pulled her close so that no-one could hear, and murmured, 'You have misread my mind, lady. I do love thee, but my duty lies elsewhere.' He kissed her then, a brief touch that scorched her mouth and buckled her knees.

Then, without looking back, he picked up his sword and strode out of the room.

'I have to go with him,' Stephen said suddenly. 'I have to say goodbye to Howell.' Howell was the best friend Stephen had ever had. The thought of never seeing Howell again, never laughing at his silly jokes and weird tales of his master's magical doings really choked him up.

'You can't go. We haven't got time,' El said urgently. Her skin prickled with hot pinpoints. Imagination spread the itch all over her body. Her desire to scratch was sending her mad. She stripped off her dress and pulled up her shift, carefully searching for fleas.

Stephen averted his eyes. 'I'll go and find Howell while you work out how to get us home.'

'Please stay, Stephen. We need you. We need all of us here so we can try to make a plan,' Callie begged. Desolation over Lancelot's going had been overtaken by concern for her sister. She'd risked El's life coming here; she couldn't bear to think that El might die because of it.

'Don't worry about Howell. Lancelot will explain to Bors what's happened to us,' Meg interposed.

'Why should he?' Callie flashed, momentarily distracted. 'Bors tried to kill him.'

'Bors will find out. And I'm sure he'll tell Howell all about it.' Meg flashed a warning glance at Callie, but her attention had shifted to El.

'Lift up your arms,' she commanded, interrupting El's urgent scratching.

Reluctantly El did so, peering at her armpits along with Callie. Stricken, they stared at each other. 'Maybe it's only a boil?' she said, contorting her body as she tried to double-check under both armpits at once.

Callie felt cold fear like a lead weight in her stomach. She held her wrist first against El's forehead and then against her own. 'You feel awfully hot,' she said anxiously. 'I think you've got a fever. Is that one of the symptoms?'

'I don't know,' El lied.

'Well, we've tried prayer, and magic, and even old magic to get us back,' said Meg, ticking them off on her fingers as she spoke. 'It looks like time's up. We'll just have to help ourselves. But I haven't got any ideas. What about the rest of you?'

'We have to think of something,' Callie said urgently. 'If El's got the plague, then we'll all get it. And unless we get medical attention soon, we'll all die.'

'Who cares.'

There was silence. Everyone looked at Lev.

'Surely you don't mean it? Surely you want to live?'

'Why? What for?'

'Because ...' Callie remembered his appearance at school, what he'd said about his gran. She couldn't think of a convincing reply.

'Because you're a knight. You're special,' Meg encouraged him.

'I'm a fake.' Lev shot a savage glance at El, who tossed her head.

'You should have more faith in yourself,' Meg told him. 'You could be special if you wanted.'

'Well, I've got to get back whether you want to or not.' El rearranged her shift, then pulled her dress on over her head. To take her mind off her itches, she set about tidying the table, rolling up the linen strips and sloshing the bloody water from the dish out the window.

'We have to go together — all of us. So has anyone got any ideas?' Meg asked. 'What about you, Stephen?'

Stephen shrugged, but didn't say anything. He propped himself against the table and stared unhappily into space, while Meg and Callie sat down on either side of Lev. Silence settled as they racked their brains for a solution.

'Please. Please, someone suggest something!' El's tongue felt swollen, furry in her dry mouth. 'Can I have a drink?' Her words sounded slurred. Alarmed, Callie poured wine into a goblet and handed it to her sister.

El drank it down in one gulp and closed her eyes. 'Thanks,' she whispered.

Callie tore off a square of linen and sloshed water onto it. She began to sponge El's forehead.

'I may have something,' Stephen said. Pushing himself away from the table, he started to pace about the room as he thought through his ideas. 'Perhaps this place isn't real, after all. Perhaps we're still in your program. Perhaps we're following the program according to the rules of the computer.'

'What do you mean?' Callie asked.

'I mean, maybe the answer lies in your program. Maybe we're forced to stay here until we've played it all out. How does the story of the Lady of Shalott end, Callie?' He stopped in front of her.

There was a moment's silence.

'With my death.'

'No!' El grabbed hold of Callie. 'That's not going to happen!'

'Did you set this up like some sort of game? Were there any rules?'

'No,' said Callie. 'I just thought of the Lady of Shalott, that's all. I used scenes from my dad's historical programs, and scanned us into them.'

'The scenes where we've been?'

'Yeah.'

'And you picked me. And Lev?'

'Yeah.' Callie blushed.

'Did you scan in anyone who isn't here now?'

'No. Everyone I scanned in, is here. But I didn't draw in any of the townspeople, or the king and queen and knights ... but I guess they were here anyway?' Callie's eyes glimmered with excitement as she began to understand which way Stephen's mind was working.

'Tell me again exactly what you put on the computer.' Stephen listened intently as she described the tower room and how they'd walked through the fields, past the river, finally travelling the narrow streets of Camelot and climbing to the castle itself.

He nodded as she came to the end of her recital. She had confirmed what he thought might be the case. But he had to find out more. 'Did you scan any other places on the computer? Anywhere we haven't been?'

'No.'

'Have we been anywhere that you didn't factor into the computer?'

'Not so far as I know.' Callie turned to El. 'Where did you go swimming?'

'Across the meadow from here.' El gestured towards the window. 'Somewhere over there.' She looked baffled. 'Why? What difference does it make?'

'I'm wondering what will happen to us if we leave the tower, and Camelot, and go to a place that Callie didn't scan into her dad's computer.'

Everyone thought through the implications.

'We could drop off into nothing,' Callie pointed out.

Stephen nodded. 'Exactly. But our lives and our future are in our hands right now and we have to make a decision. If we don't leave, we'll probably get sick and die here. But if we follow my plan, we might just escape … or we might drop into a void, become trapped in nowhere. Which means we die anyway. You have to decide if you're willing to take the risk.'

'I will. I don't have any choice,' said El.

'And I'm not letting you go alone,' said Callie. 'But if Stephen's right, just think — we could zap straight home to the twenty-first century!'

'It's too dangerous,' Meg objected.

'I don't think we have much choice,' said Stephen.

'Where would we go?' El asked. 'I mean, how do we go about stumbling off the edge of the world as Callie designed it?'

Stephen shrugged. 'I guess we walk out of here and just keep on going.'

'I started this. I think I should finish it.'

Everyone looked at Callie, wondering what she had in mind. She tried to explain. 'I mean, I'm supposed to be the Lady of Shalott, right? And we all know what happened to her.'

'I don't,' said Lev.

> '"Down she came and found a boat.
> Beneath a willow left afloat …"'

'She lay down in a boat and floated down to Camelot. And on the way, she died,' Meg interrupted Callie.

'No! You can't do that. I won't let you,' cried El.

'You can't stop me.' Callie said calmly. 'Think about it. We'll go down to the river and find a boat. Lev has to be my boatman because it was Elaine of Astolat's brother, Sir Lavaine, who took her body down to Camelot. The rest of you had better hide, but I'll lie down, just like she did in the poem, and pretend I'm dead. We'll float down to Camelot and —'

'Off the edge of the world?' Meg looked frightened.

'A bit like those sailors who thought the world was flat and that they'd fall off the edge if they were blown off course. Except we hope it'll get us home.' Stephen surveyed them. 'I think Callie's idea is a good one. I mean, she set up the Lady of Shalott and the court of King Arthur on the computer, so perhaps we have to follow the program through to its logical conclusion.'

'Which means the Lady of Shalott dies!' El said fiercely.

'No, I won't,' Callie protested.

'We'll probably all die if we stay,' Stephen pointed out. 'So what do you think? Are you willing to try?'

'Camelot's built on an estuary. What if we get caught in a current and we're washed out to sea? We'll have no food or water. No shelter, or anything.' El's headache was getting worse. She felt like she was burning up.

'How far beyond Camelot did you scan?'

Callie thought about it. 'I scanned in everything between Camelot and this tower, and I stopped where you see that road vanishing over the hill behind us.' She gestured towards the window.

'But we're not going that way. We're going down the river towards the sea. And we'll know soon enough if it's going to work. If nothing's happened by the time we pass Camelot, we'll turn round and try to row back,' said Stephen.

'But if we exist only in the bit that Callie's scanned, we might get zapped into nothing,' Meg said again.

Stephen shrugged. 'I told you it was a risk. It's up to you.' He stood up and stretched. 'But I don't care if we don't go. We can stay here, if you like, and take our chances.' He half-hoped they'd agree. He was happy here. He had mates. The pressure of the HSC was off him. So was his responsibility of living up to his parents' expectations. Besides, he liked the life of the court. It would be good to earn a knighthood so that he too could take part in tournaments and hunting parties.

'No.' Callie cast a worried glance at El. 'We have to go. We really should leave as soon as possible.'

'What if you die in the boat, just like the Lady of

Shalott? It's too much of a risk. If you can't think of anything else, I vote we stay here,' El insisted.

'I won't die,' Callie answered with a calmness she didn't feel. 'I'll make sure I don't. But I think we're right to try to do it this way, to take it to the end, seeing everything else in the poem seems to have happened. I mean, the mirror breaking, and the "web" flying out the window, and all the rest of it.'

'Then I hope there's a boat waiting for us under a willow tree. Otherwise we're really stuffed.' Meg sounded despondent.

'Let's stop arguing and get on with it.' Now that the time had come to make a move, Callie was desperate to be gone. She knew the swellings in El's armpits were too big and too dark for boils. El needed medical attention urgently. And the sooner they left, the sooner she could try to forget Lancelot. It was agony to think of him hurrying through Camelot on his way back to the castle, moving further and further out of her life. Once she was back in the twenty-first century, maybe she'd get over him. She knew she never would if she stayed here. She understood now why the Lady of Shalott hadn't been able to face life without him.

'What about the other people living here? We can't just leave them.'

A brief silence greeted Meg's observation. In their haste to save themselves, they'd forgotten the servants who kept the tower in order, awaiting the lord and lady's return.

'You heard Lancelot. The plague's already spread through the tower,' El pointed out.

'But they don't all need to get sick, not if they stay away from the rats.'

'Maybe that old woman could try some black magic on them.' Impatient to be gone, El walked across to the door and propped herself against it.

'But they'd be safer if they left the tower. Maybe they could all go to the river and wash their clothes and themselves to get rid of the fleas.'

'So long as they keep away from Camelot afterwards,' Callie added fiercely.

'They'll have to. The fires will keep them out.'

'They'll never leave here just because we tell them to.'

Everyone thought about it.

'They would if the tower was on fire,' Lev said unexpectedly. 'We can set a fire up here, and then warn them to get out and go down to the river. We can tell them to get in because the water is the safest place to be. Then the fleas will drown and —'

'And the fire will destroy all the rats!' Callie cried eagerly. 'That's a brilliant idea, Lev.'

'Maybe we should set a ring of fire around the tower too, just to catch any rats that try to escape?' he suggested, looking pleased with himself. Going out in a blaze of fire might be a good way to go. Just like those old Vikings his teacher in primary school had been so keen on. He didn't think sailing off into nothing was such a great idea. In fact, it sounded pretty damn crazy to him.

'If rats abandon sinking ships, I guess they'll abandon burning towers,' Callie agreed.

'You've finally given us a good reason for bringing you here, Lev.' As soon as she said the words, El regretted them. But she felt so hot, and her head was so sore, it was hard to think rationally.

Lev's face contorted with rage. 'I'll show you!' he hissed.

'Come and help us collect some wood,' Meg said quickly, grabbing Lev's arm, trying to defuse the situation.

'It's pitch dark outside,' Stephen objected.

'We can't waste any time.' Callie was desperate to be on the move.

'Who's going to set the fire inside?' El opened the door.

'I am.' Lev gave her a murderous glare.

'Let's do it together,' Meg suggested.

'I'll do it by myself.'

Callie looked at Lev, and suddenly understood that he really needed this chance to prove himself, prove that he could be as brave and noble as all the other knights at court. She remembered how they'd joked about him, saying what a no-hoper he was, but that coming to Camelot and meeting the lady might save him. Instead, he might die a terrible death; they all might.

'We'll get everything ready and then you can start the fire in here. We'll wait until everyone's out before we light the fires outside,' Stephen suggested.

'Okay.' Lev shrugged. He felt nervous — but resolute. He'd show them he wasn't the loser everyone thought he was.

'We won't start the fire until we make sure you're safe,' said Callie. 'And Lev — if we get back okay, we'll help you turn your life around, I promise.'

'There's so much you can do, if you've got the courage to take a chance.' Meg remembered Lev's angry outburst in the chapel. She wondered if he believed in God, and if the praying and chanting had helped him. But really, it was more important to make Lev believe in himself right now.

'We'll help you find a job, and somewhere to live. Things will be different, you'll see.'

'We're wasting time,' Callie said impatiently. 'Give me a hand with this.' She took hold of the cupboard and tried to drag it towards the bed. She heaved and strained, but it was surprisingly heavy.

'I'll do that.' Stephen moved towards Callie. 'Lev can help me. Maybe you can start piling up the smaller stuff?'

'Do you think the tower will burn all right?'

'Sure.' Stephen looked at the furniture, the wood panelling, the hanging tapestries, the woven rugs on the floor. 'This stuff will go up like gum trees in a bushfire.'

'Can I take my lute?' Without waiting for an answer, Meg picked up the big-bellied instrument and stroked it with a loving hand.

'I'm taking my mobile phone.' Stephen walked to the bed and felt under the bolster.

'And I'll take my paintbox. And the diamond Lancelot gave me.' Callie pulled the shining gem from her purse, tucked it into the box and hefted it under her arm.

'I've got nothing to take.' El gave an uncomfortable laugh. 'No talents to speak of.'

'Except your knowledge of the plague and first aid, and lots of useful stuff like that,' Callie comforted her.

'You were the first to try to help when that knight was poisoned at the dinner table,' added Meg. 'And you looked after Lev, and you dressed Lancelot's wound. And you didn't pass out once.'

'I guess I didn't have time to think about it. No-one else knew what to do.' El looked slightly happier.

Stephen tucked his mobile phone into the waistband of his trousers and held out the discman to Lev. 'Do you want this?'

'Yeah, sure. Maybe I can flog it when I get back.' Lev sounded thoroughly depressed.

As they moved the furniture, Callie felt her stomach shrink into a small knot of fear. She was sure something terrible was about to happen. And it was all her fault. She had started this and it was too late now to stop it. They had to keep on going, but where would their journey take them? To freedom? Or to death?

CHAPTER ELEVEN

The barricade was in place, ready to be fired. Lev looked down at it from high up in the tower room and noticed Callie. She looked like a small red ant in the scarlet dress, a pinprick of colour in the grey light of early dawn.

He should get on with it; start the fire then hurry down to warn the servants. They'd have no time to gather their belongings, but it was just as well. Their gear would be better off burnt, along with the rats and the fleas.

Still he lingered, reluctant to set the final scene in motion. There was a soft scratching from the parapet above. Lev craned his head upwards and saw a pigeon puffing out its chest, cooing its own self-importance. He picked up some crumbs of mouldy cheese from the floor and threw them up at the sky. There was a flutter of beating wings as the flock dived on them.

Easy for a pigeon, Lev thought. No need to question the why and how of living. Just get on and do what you have to do. Like I should be doing right now.

The fat candle and tapers El had lit for her ritual were almost burnt down, but she had brought extra tapers from the kitchen, to be saved for other long, dark nights. They lay in a bundle on the squat cupboard. One by one, Lev lit them from the sputtering flame of the fat candle. He approached the bed. He wished he had paper to crumple up to make the fire really go. It was important to set such a blaze that the rats would burn before they could escape into the surrounding countryside.

Carefully, he touched the taper to the thin fabric hanging around the bed. It ignited into multiple tongues of flame. Lev pushed the table closer, then heaved the two wooden benches on top of the blazing bedclothes.

Clutching the lighted tapers, he held his breath against the smoke as he clattered to the door and out across the passage to the room opposite. His armour was heavy and restricted his movements. Maybe he should change out of it? But no. If he was going to do something heroic, he ought to be dressed for the part.

He fired the bed where Stephen had slept then scrambled down the stone steps and into the next set of rooms. Smoke swirled around him as he went on down, treading carefully, almost tripping over rats that seemed to pour from every crevice. He pushed a hand over his nose and rushed to a window for a gulp of fresh air.

Callie stood beyond the barricade, watching for him. As soon as his head appeared, she waved a lighted taper in the air and hopped up and down to attract his attention. She jerked her thumb to the right several times and shouted something. Lev couldn't hear what she was saying, but he waved back to her. To his surprise, she touched the taper to the pile of wood then, setting it alight. The others seemed to be waiting for her signal. As Lev watched, several pinpoints of light flickered along the makeshift barricade. He had no idea why they'd decided to start the fire so soon; he just knew he'd have to hurry.

Abandoning the rest of the rooms, he moved on down past the dining hall towards the kitchen and scullery. Long tendrils of smoke swirled around him, like ghostly fingers beckoning him to the conflagration. The chain mail felt hot and uncomfortable, but he couldn't take time now to pull it off.

The kitchen was deserted, although fires blazed in the hearth and huge iron cooking pots bubbled above them. Overlying the rich smell of stew was the bitter tang of burnt bread.

'Hey!' he shouted. 'Is anyone here?' He listened, but there was no sound of human voices. He stumbled on through the storerooms and cellar towards a flight of stone steps that led down into darkness. Surely the servants must be here somewhere?

He called again, and was answered by a shout. He clattered down the last few stairs and stopped, dismayed at the sight of the small, damp stone cells that made up the servants' living quarters. They were all down there, panicky and confused as they scurried to and fro, squabbling over their few possessions and who had the right to them. For the first time, Lev realised the consequences of their decision, that they were destroying the very little that these people had: their home, their possessions and their livelihood.

It's to save their lives. Lev tried to comfort himself with the thought as he shouted, 'The tower's on fire! Quick! You have to get out of here!' He grabbed the fat old cook by the arm, sensing the others would follow if he could just set someone in motion. 'Run for your lives!'

'We cannot leave our chattels behind.' Despite her awe of the unknown knight, the cook shook him off and stood square in his path, clutching her meagre bundle to her chest.

'There's no time for that!' Lev shoved her towards the stairs, beckoning the others to follow. He raised his voice, coughing as he breathed in the smoke that had started to swirl more densely about them. 'Camelot is also on fire. You cannot go there. You must go to the river. It's the safest place. Get into the river and stay in the water until you see that the fire has gone out.'

Alarmed by his shouts and the billowing smoke, the old woman heaved herself up the stairs as fast as her bulk would allow. ''Tis a curse,' she panted as she climbed. 'We shall all die.'

'Go to the river,' Lev shouted, as the other servants swarmed behind her, all jostling to get in front. 'You won't die if you do as I say!'

There were yells and curses as bodies blocked the passage. Together they scrambled to get to the door that would take them out to safety.

Lev saw them as far as the kitchen, then clattered back down the stairs, shouting a warning just in case he'd missed anyone. But he could hear nothing other than the dull boom of the fire as it ate through the tower above him. Smoke choked him. It made his eyes water but dried his mouth and lungs. He climbed back to the kitchen to search for a jug of water; anything to slake his thirst.

Bunches of dried herbs caught his eye. He set fire to

them, inhaling their sweet fragrance as the storeroom behind him erupted in flame. He lurched through the kitchen towards the dining hall, touching the lighted tapers to everything in sight. 'Oh Lord, *start a fire* ...' The words ran through his mind. He wasn't sure where he'd heard the tune before, but he hummed softly to himself as the laden table blazed up, sending out a spicy smell of barbecue. '*Let me burn, burn again,*' he sang as he stumbled back towards the kitchen.

Smoke swirled thicker and he could hardly see where he was going now. It was time to get out of the tower. Where was the passage? Where was the door? He stumbled on. Fiery golden arms followed him, coming closer, reaching out to him. He felt their fierce caress through the chainmail. The heat burnt his skin. He flung himself forward. His searching fingers scrabbled over smooth stone. No passage. No doorway.

Suddenly afraid, he spun around looking for a gap, a break that would lead him to safety. He darted for a patch of darkness, only to find a wall of fire beyond. He stared at the flames, mesmerised by their savage ferocity. He had done his job too well. The fire would kill him as well as the rats. But he'd got the servants out of the tower. He would be a hero now. No matter what happened, he would have earned his knighthood.

There! A sudden draught, the fire blazed up, sending the smoke swirling higher. In the shift, Lev saw a dark outline in the stone wall. Consumed by fear, he ran down the passage towards the burning door, whacking it open with his bare hands.

The pain made him gasp. But he was outside now and he bent over, choking and gasping for breath.

'Callie!' He pulled himself upright with an effort, listening intently for an answering cry. But he heard only the roar of the flames and the popping and spitting of dry, burning wood. 'Callie!'

A ring of fire surrounded the tower, a high blazing wall that imprisoned him. It was creeping closer all the time as dry summer grass ignited before it. He began to run, searching for a break.

Callie had said they'd wait for him before setting the barricade alight. Why had they lit it so early? Then he remembered the tide of rats flooding down the stairs, and understood.

'Meg!' he yelled. 'Stephen!' He felt real fear now. He called again and again, but only the voice of the fire answered him.

Callie had shouted something, had jerked her thumb to the right before starting the fire. Surely that meant they'd left a gap for him and the servants to escape? But where was it? He circled the tower, pressing himself flat against the walls as he searched for the window he'd stood at earlier.

There it was! He positioned himself underneath, so he could replay Callie's movements, so he could understand her directions. Once more he began to run inside the ring of fire, heavy and awkward in his metal prison, searching frantically. And then he saw it: a dark hole in the flaming barrier.

'*Oh lord, start a fire. Lift me up, lift me higher* …' He hunched over and pulled his visor down to protect his face. Curling himself into a ball, he launched himself at the small space.

A sudden roar deafened him as the barricade collapsed, shooting sparks high into the air. He was trapped now, trapped within the fiery circle. And the flames were coming closer all the time.

'I'm not leaving till we've found Lev.' Meg leaned on her heavy stick and wiped her sweating forehead. The argument had raged for some time, but she still hoped against all odds that Lev would somehow find a way out.

'He won't come,' Stephen said flatly, switching his stick from hand to hand as he kept an eye open for escaping rats. 'He can't. There's no place for him to get through.'

'But we can't just leave him here to die!' El was close to tears. All she could think of was Lev's shining face, his pride when Meg had introduced him as 'Sir Lavaine'. And her own mean intervention. Lev had nothing, yet she'd made sure she'd taken this from him too. And because of it, even though he knew how dangerous it was, he'd offered to set fire to the tower so he could prove his bravery to them all, so he could show them he was worth a knighthood.

It would be her fault if he died. She couldn't get away from it. All her life she'd tried to be the best, even if it meant putting everyone else down so that she could look good. She'd done it with Lev. And she'd always done it with Callie.

Why? Why was it so important to get the better of her sister? Jealousy?

El threw down her stick and clapped her hands over her ears, trying to block out the knowledge of how much she resented Callie's resemblance to their mother, and her father's special treatment of her because of it. How badly she'd treated Callie. And Lev. 'Please don't let him die,' she whispered.

'Are you feeling all right?' Callie touched her arm, looking concerned.

El shook her head. She felt sick and frightened. But the over-riding feeling was shame. She wanted to apologise to her sister, apologise to Lev, apologise to everyone she'd ever hurt.

Callie gave her a quick hug. 'Don't worry. We'll leave just as soon as Lev turns up,' she said with a confidence she didn't feel. 'I told him where we'd leave the gap. He gave me a wave; he understood what I meant. And the servants found it all right, so there's no reason why Lev shouldn't. He'll be here any minute now.'

'The gap's gone. You saw the barricade collapse,' said Stephen.

'He'll find another way through. He might have to wait until the fire dies down.' Meg took a couple of quick steps and brought her heavy stick down with a crash. 'Gotcha!' She looked down at the mangled remains of the rat with satisfaction.

Trying to ignore her nagging conscience, El started to scratch again, her prickly skin inflamed by the heat of the fire.

'We'll have you in hospital getting treatment before you know it.' Callie was torn between not wanting to abandon Lev and a growing fear for El. She had mentioned a headache. Callie was sure El was much sicker than she was letting on. She kept an arm around her sister. What would she do if anything happened to El?

She shook her head, numb with misery. She couldn't believe things had gone so wrong. This wasn't what she'd planned at all. She'd set the scene, but then the program had taken on a life of its own, a life over which she had no control. 'What if?' she'd kept asking her father. Now she knew. For better or worse, intervention changed things, no matter whether it was history or a legend like this one. And the greatest test was still ahead of them. If Stephen's idea didn't work, they would all die.

'Wait! I can see something.' Meg flung down her stick and ran towards the small gap opening up once again in the barricade.

'Lev!' She pointed a shaking finger as a scorched figure catapulted through the hole in the fiery wall and landed at their feet.

'Lev!' Callie echoed as she raced to his side. 'We thought we'd lost you. I mean, we thought you were dead!' she babbled as she helped him up.

'You were nearly right.' He pulled up his visor and gave her a shaky grin. His teeth gleamed white in his smoke-blackened face.

'You've made a real mess of your armour. It's lucky you don't need it any more.' There was no jealousy, only relief in Stephen's voice as he surveyed Lev's scorched and dented metal suit. 'Well done, mate. Glad you're safe.'

'Are you all right, Lev? Can you walk okay?'

Callie glanced across at El, surprised to see her sister in tears. 'We have to hurry,' she urged. 'We've got to get El to hospital.'

Lev looked at her. For a moment Callie thought he was going to refuse to come. Then he said, 'Yeah, I'm okay. Let's get going.'

Callie fetched her paintbox and tucked it under her arm, linking her other arm through El's for support.

'What about the servants? Did they all manage to escape?' Lev asked as they set off towards the river.

'Yes, thanks to you,' said Stephen.

'Even the fat cook,' Meg added with a grin. 'But she wasn't too happy about leaving all her stuff behind.' She patted her lute, glad she'd been able to save it from the fire. Briefly, she closed her eyes, summoning up the music of the monks. As the voices soared in her memory she relaxed slightly, feeling comforted.

'Lancelot was wrong.' Saying his name sent a stab of pain through Callie's heart, but she continued bravely. 'If the cook really was Morgan le Fay she'd have changed herself into an owl and just flown away or something.'

'The cook wasn't the only one in the kitchen,' El chimed in, remembering the shadowy figure she'd seen hiding behind the others. 'It may have been Morgan's magic that started all this. I know the old woman seemed frightened of her. I reckon lots of them still believe in the old ways and practise magic.'

'And lots of them are Christian,' Meg retorted.

'Well, modern medicine's what we need right now,' Callie said briskly.

El nodded agreement. Her eyes, nose and throat felt raw from the smoke of the fire. Hammers pounded in her brain. She was burning with fever. All she wanted to do was lie down and rest her aching limbs, but she kept trudging on. The path was rough, obscured in parts by drifting mist. It was as if they were walking on clouds, tramping through a grey vacuum. She felt as though she'd been walking forever.

A wall of dark trees loomed out of the mist. As the forest closed over their heads, the path disappeared, lost in the black gloom. Drifts of leaves softened their footfalls and clung wetly to their ankles. Unseen brambles reached out, snagging clothes and skin as they passed by.

The sullen dawn yielded to a stormy morning and the mist began to clear. The trees thinned out, revealing the reedy banks of the river where herons strutted, scavenging for breakfast, and ducklings followed their mother in an early morning swim.

'So where's this boat supposed to be?' Stephen asked.

'It's over there! Look. Underneath the willow tree, just like the poem said.' Callie gestured down the river to a long, flat wooden barge with a black linen cover.

'Before you go, I have something to tell you,' Lev said unexpectedly.

Puzzled, Callie turned to him. She was impatient to be gone, but there was the same note in Lev's voice that she'd heard when he'd announced his determination to stay in the tower and set it on fire.

'I've decided not to come back with you,' Lev told them. 'I'm going to stay here in Camelot.'

'But you can't!' Callie cried.

'Why not?' He surveyed their anxious faces.

Callie remembered again her father's warning not to meddle. With all her heart she wished she'd istened to him, wished that they were all safely home. Instead El was sick, possibly dying. She herself felt torn between wanting to be with Lancelot and needing to stay with El. And now Lev was trying to change things too. But she couldn't let him stay. She had to change his mind. 'We can't just leave you here,' she said. 'What would you do? Where would you go?'

'To Camelot.' Lev turned and pointed to the walls of the town. 'I swore an oath to protect Arthur at the knighthood ceremony. I'm a member of Arthur's court now.' He swung back to face Callie. 'It's different for you. You've got families waiting for you, but I've got nothing in the twenty-first century. There's no place for me there.'

'But someone will miss you, surely?'

Lev thought about it. 'Nuh,' he said. 'There's no-one there who cares about me.'

'But we'll help you —'

'It's much better for me here,' Lev interrupted Callie's protest. 'Coming close to death has made me see things differently. I'm a knight here. People respect me, and I'm going to make sure I'm worthy of their respect, that I become worthy of knighthood.'

'You've already proved that,' Callie reassured him. 'You got all those people out of the tower.'

'You're a hero, Lev. You deserve to be a knight,' El added quickly.

He grinned at the twins. 'Don't worry about me. I can have a good life here. I'll learn how to ride and take part in the tournaments and hunting. And if the time comes, I'll even fight for King Arthur against Mordred.'

Listening to Lev spell out what he himself had thought, Stephen was tempted to stay on as well. But he acknowledged Lev was right. No-one would miss Lev, whereas his family would move heaven and earth to find him if he stayed behind. There was some comfort in the thought.

'Good luck then,' he said, nodding at Lev. 'I wish I could stay with you.'

Me too, Callie added silently, still grieving for Lancelot. Then she looked at her sister. 'Time to go,' she said briskly and threw her arms around Lev. 'Take care,' she said. 'I guess you're going to become part of the legend too.'

'Maybe you'll read about me when you get home?' Lev laughed at the idea.

'I already have,' Callie said seriously. 'You're Sir Lavaine, my brother — remember?' A thought checked her. 'But I need you to be my boatman,' she said anxiously. 'Sir Lavaine, Elaine of Astolat's brother, took her down to Camelot.'

'I can do that,' Stephen offered. 'I'm also supposed to be your brother.'

Callie looked from one to the other. 'But it has to be right.'

'It has to *look* right,' Stephen corrected. He flashed a grin at Lev. 'Let's swap clothes. You can tell the court you lost your armour in the fire. Maybe Arthur will give you a shiny new set in gratitude for stopping the plague from spreading to Camelot.'

'But they'll know,' Callie cried. 'As soon as they see Lev, they'll know it wasn't him in the boat with me.'

'By then we'll be gone, one way or another,' said Stephen. The thought sent a chill through them all.

'Okay, let's do it,' said Lev.

'Come on, El.' As Callie led her sister down to the boat, Stephen and Lev undressed.

'Will you tell Howell we had to go?' Stephen asked as he struggled into Lev's blackened armour. 'He already knows most of the story. Please tell him I had no time to say goodbye.'

'I'll do that. But I won't go to the castle until you're safely away.' Lev stepped into Stephen's breeches, then pulled on the stockings. They were far too big for his thin frame. He hoped they wouldn't fall down and embarrass him at court. 'Are you going to get home all right? Do you think your plan will work?' he asked.

Stephen shrugged. 'I guess you'll never know,' he said and turned away.

'Lean on me, El.' Callie helped her sister onto the boat and surveyed her anxiously. 'You look awful. Why don't you stretch out along the seat there?' She laid her wrist against her sister's forehead. It was burning hot. El's face was white and sheened with sweat, although the early morning air was cool. 'Lie down,' Callie urged. 'You can pretend to be me. Meg and I will hide.'

'I don't have to pretend.' El stretched out along the wooden seat, easing her aching joints with a grateful sigh. 'I really am Elaine of Astolat.'

And you're dying! All the colour fled from Callie's face. She gave a little gasp and bit down hard on her lip, battling to keep her thoughts to herself. 'Come on!' she called urgently. 'We've got to go.' She thrust the long paddle into Stephen's hands, then pulled Meg into the centre of the boat. They carefully stashed the paintbox and the lute under the seat then lay down, covering themselves with the black cloth.

Stephen untied the boat from its anchoring tree and, using the long pole, pushed it away from the river bank. Following the current, they began to drift slowly towards Camelot while Stephen dipped the pole at intervals to keep the boat on course.

'Aren't you supposed to sing or something?' Meg whispered from under the covering.

There was no reply from the front of the boat.

'El!' Callie called, panicking.

'I can't sing. I've got a terrible voice,' El mumbled.

'I'll do it then.' Callie thought for a moment, then began a lament to Lancelot:

'Oh, you keep on turning
Oh, you keep me burning,
Burning in the fires of hell ...'

Her voice choked up. She couldn't continue.

'You say you'll never leave me
You say you won't deceive me
But you don't really love me, I can tell.'

El finished the lament.

'What's that supposed to be?' Stephen had his free hand to his head, trying unsuccessfully to block both ears at once.

'It's the latest hit,' El said huffily.

'I'd never have known.' Stephen glanced from El to the two bumps underneath the black linen.

'Well, gee, thanks. Why don't you sing then if you're so bloody good?'

'I'll do it,' Meg offered, lifting the covering slightly.

'Good idea,' Stephen said quickly. 'Thanks, Meg.'

'Our father, God Celestial,
Now are we come to pray to thee,
We are thy children, therefore we call,
Hear us Father, mercifully.'

Meg's clear, sweet voice rang out in an archaic version of the Lord's Prayer.

'That's beautiful. Do you sing that at your church?' Callie asked, as the last notes died away.

'No. We sang it here, at Lev's knighthood ceremony. I thought it would be a good way to say goodbye to him.'

'You've got a great voice. Are you a professional singer?'

'No,' Meg answered Stephen. 'But I've decided I'm going to study music when I leave school. So I can find out more about it, about the music of the past. It's what I want to do with my life.'

'I didn't know that,' El mumbled.

'Neither did I until recently,' Meg admitted. 'I think it's linked to my coming to Camelot, and learning to play the lute and listening to the music here. I didn't realise how intricate and beautiful music could be.' She hesitated, wondering if they would laugh at her if she told them how she really felt. She decided to take a chance. 'It's a bit hard to explain,' she said, 'but the whole time we've been here I've been making comparisons, and questioning what we do in the twenty-first century. How we live, what we believe, our values — stuff like that.'

'And have you come to any conclusions?'

Meg was relieved that Stephen sounded as if he really wanted to know.

'Not really. I just think there's more to our being here than we realise. And I just hate it that we don't seem to care about anyone but ourselves. I mean, look how Lancelot knows everything that's going on here and they don't even have phones.'

'Camelot's a lot smaller than where we come from,' Callie pointed out.

'Yeah, and we have television and the Internet to keep us in touch with the whole world.' Meg struggled to explain herself. 'I mean, we know there are wars and famines and disasters going on. And we know that people are dying because of them. But what do we care? We sit and watch it on television like it's all a movie. We chat to pretend friends on the Internet and we think we're in touch with reality, but all we're doing is having relationships with machines!'

'Life wasn't so good in the Middle Ages either,' said Stephen, adding, 'Especially for the lower classes.'

'I can't do anything about them, but I can try and do something about what's going on in our own world,' Meg retorted.

'Like what?'

Meg thought about it. 'I don't have the answers. All I know is that music is the key for me. When I heard those monks singing in the chapel, I felt as though I was coming close to understanding what life's all about. It was almost like hearing the voice of God.'

'Music's not going to end wars or feed the hungry!'

'In a way it will. Music's a universal language. It crosses over race and nations and religions, that's why it's so powerful. And that's why I want to study it when we get back.'

'If we get back,' Stephen interposed.

'*When* we get back,' Meg corrected him. 'I'm going to become a musician, maybe even compose my own stuff. I'm going to bring music to people, and hope it helps to bring peace.'

The wind had picked up. It pushed them faster down the river, accompanying their passage with a mournful whine. Callie shifted uncomfortably. The boards were hard beneath her back. She felt damp and cold.

'We're coming close to Camelot,' Stephen warned.

'Good. I feel as though we've been in this bloody boat for hours,' El grumbled.

'How are you doing?' Callie called.

'I'm okay.' El felt like she was dying, like the real Lady of Shalott, but there was no way she'd tell that to Callie.

But Callie knew. She lay still at the bottom of the boat, grieving and desperate. Her heart thumped in her chest. *Ba-boom. Ba-boom.* Like a clock ticking away the last seconds of their lives. Memories of her father, and Gran, and Honey flooded her mind. Would she ever see them again? And her mother? Would she learn of their disappearance? Would she care?

I haven't lived yet, Callie thought. I haven't learned how. Things will be different if we manage to get back. She made herself a silent promise, and then wondered if she would remember to keep it. What if the memory of Camelot was erased as they came back through time?

'Please let me remember,' Callie whispered, trying to bargain with whoever might be listening. 'Even if the others forget all about this, even if they've never been here at all, I know what's happened to us has made a difference. Please help me use that knowledge to help us all.'

'What are you muttering about under there?' Stephen lifted the pole out of the river and rested briefly.

The barge was moving fast now, caught in the current that would take them past Camelot and out to sea. Or home. Or to oblivion. Callie felt her throat constrict with fear. 'Nothing,' she whispered.

'Lancelot's followed your instructions, El. Fires are burning around the city walls,' said Stephen.

Callie sniffed the fire's smoky breath. She peeked out from under the linen shroud, risking a quick glance. The sky was on fire, red and inflamed. Gritty flakes of ash settled on the barge. She put a hand to her nose, breathing through her fingers.

Fiery ripples reflected in the dark water as the barge sped on. There was a growl of thunder; lightning forked through the sky revealing the high walls of the castle, and the lords and ladies who lined the wharf below, silently watching their progress. The crowd parted to make way for Arthur and Guinevere. Lancelot followed them. He moved quickly to the edge of the wharf and peered intently at the barge.

'The Lady Charlotte!' His despairing cry rang out above the sudden babble of voices as people exclaimed and leaned closer to see for themselves.

It took all Callie's willpower not to leap out from her hiding place, to shout out reassurance to Lancelot that she was still alive. She wanted to jump out of the boat and swim to him, but she squeezed her eyes tight shut, wishing she could as easily erase him from her memory as from her sight.

'Howell!' She heard Stephen's whisper, and risked another quick glance.

The dark youth stood beside his short, barrel-chested master. Stephen waved and he returned the gesture, but uncertainly, not recognising him in Lev's armour.

'We're almost past Camelot,' Stephen said quietly then. 'Shouldn't we say goodbye, just in case we don't make it?'

'Have we saved Camelot?' Meg asked quickly. 'Have you done what you wanted, Callie?'

'No, it all went wrong.' Callie sounded desolate. 'Dad was right. I should never have tried to interfere.'

'We've stopped the plague from reaching Camelot,' El tried to comfort her.

'But we're taking it back to the twenty-first century.'

'They'll know how to deal with it there,' said Stephen.

'I warned Mordred about the snake at the Battle of Camlann,' said Meg. She remembered Mordred's longing look at Guinevere and sighed, wishing she could believe her warning would make a difference.

'We did what we could,' said Stephen. 'I think we might have helped. At least Lev seems happy with his new life.'

The boat kicked as the current of the estuary met the turbulence of the sea. It juddered and swirled around, foundering in the deep water.

'We're there,' said Stephen. 'Goodbye.' His voice faded into silence as a wave slapped against the boat, its spray drenching them all.

'I'm so sorry!' Callie cried frantically. 'I'm so sorry …'

She was choked into silence as another wave spun the boat around. It bucked and tipped them all into the water. The sea rolled over them, cradling them in its icy arms.

Callie felt herself being sucked down into darkness, spinning around and around in long, slow circles, spiralling through emptiness. She was falling, falling into nothing. Falling.

chapter twelve

Icy darkness melted into grey warmth. Callie stretched out a tentative hand and encountered the warm skin of a bare leg. Her eyes flashed open. She was lying sprawled across the motion platform. Her head ached with a rhythmic pounding, like a drum in a heavy metal band. El was crouched beside her.

'Are you all right?' Callie demanded, as her eyes focused on her sister's face.

'Of course I'm all right. It's you we're worried about. Are you okay?'

Callie nodded, feeling a wave of misery and joy

flood through her. They were back! They'd made it! And she could remember everything that had happened. She had found Lancelot — and lost him. She looked around the room, just in case by some wild chance he'd come with them. But she could see only El, Meg and herself.

'Where's Stephen?'

'Who?'

'Stephen.' And then, as they continued to look blankly at her, 'Stephen, who came with us to Camelot.'

'Camelot?' Meg echoed.

'You've had a really bad bang on the head. Maybe you should go and lie down?' El looked worried.

'Maybe you should go and lie down!' Callie retorted. 'We should send for a doctor. If you've got the plague —'

'What?' El burst out laughing. 'Callie, we live in the twenty-first century, not the Middle Ages!'

'I know.' Callie shook her head, trying to make sense of what had happened to them. 'I know.' She thought back to Camelot as she'd seen it last: ringed with fire, the light illuminating the anxious faces of the court. Lancelot calling out her name …

No! She couldn't bear to think about him.

'Where's Stephen?' she asked again, as she sat up and looked around her. 'Didn't he make it back?'

'Back from where? What are you talking about?'

Could they really not know? Callie pointed at the computer screen. But it was blank. Every trace of Camelot had been erased.

'I'm so sorry,' said Meg. Her face was pale as she helped Callie to her feet. 'You must have deleted everything when you fell just now.'

'Just now?'

Feeling as if she was moving through a dream, Callie stepped up to the computer. She hit a couple of buttons and the familiar menus came up. But she couldn't access Camelot. No matter what she tried, all trace of it had gone. She whirled to confront Meg. 'What happened when I fell?' she asked urgently. 'Tell me what you remember.'

'Well, we were fighting over this photo of Greg.' Meg pointed at the crumpled photograph lying on the floor beside Callie.

'El pushed me. I lost my balance and crashed into you, pushing you against the motion platform. I saw you grabbing at levers and buttons as you went down. I don't know if you were trying to save the program or break your fall, but the computer lit up and sort of fizzed. Then the screen went blank. You hit your head as you fell, and you've been out of it ever since.' Nervously, Meg fiddled with the ring in her nose.

'We've been shaking you and shouting at you, but you were out cold,' El chimed in. 'Actually, we were getting really worried about you. I was just about to call a doctor.'

'We were worried about your program too. All that hard work …' Meg's voice faltered into guilty silence.

Callie glanced quickly around the workroom. Her paintbox was in the same place, and closed, just as she remembered leaving it. She stumbled across to it and flung open the lid, holding her breath in expectation.

No diamond. No clue to tell her if what had happened was real, or a dream.

No, not a dream. Not with the image of Lancelot so vivid in her mind. She could still feel the roughness of chain mail under her fingertips and the touch of his lips on hers. Her whole body ached with the pain of memory.

She closed her eyes. Lancelot's image, sharp as a photograph, flashed before her. But, like a photograph, surely the image would fade in time and so would the crushing sense of desolation? Surely she would remember only the joy of loving and being loved by the finest knight in Arthur's realm?

Yes, she had done what she'd set out to do after all. The result wasn't what she'd wanted, or even expected, but at least she had tried. And the knowledge she had gained would never leave her.

She grabbed El's arm. 'What about Lev?' she asked urgently.

'The loser from school? What about him?' Despite her casual dismissal, El looked uncomfortable.

'Don't you remember?' Callie pressed her.

'Remember what? You're acting really weird.'

Callie turned and pressed her fingertips against the blank screen, feeling an infinite sense of relief. The plague, the fire, Lev. They hadn't left him behind after all. None of it had really happened. 'It's all over,' she said softly. 'No harm's been done.'

'But your program's gone!' El looked bewildered. 'And it's all my fault. We shouldn't have butted in when you didn't want us. I'm sorry, Callie.'

'It doesn't matter,' said Callie, wondering if she'd ever heard El apologising for anything before. 'I've finished with Camelot. I don't need it any more.' She inspected Meg and El closely. But they seemed the same as usual in their crumpled school uniforms. Nothing had changed. She looked down at herself, half-expecting to see the long red silk dress, or even the green gown she'd first worn as the Lady of Shalott. But she saw only her uniform, with its faded line around the skirt where the hem had been let down. They had all come back, then — but had any of them been anywhere?

'Why don't you need Camelot any more?' Meg stepped closer to Callie, inspecting her with a worried frown.

Because I've been there. Meg's question was easy

enough to answer, if she was prepared to say the words aloud. And how they'd laugh at her if she did. So she said only, 'I've proved to myself that I can do what I want to do on this.' She tapped the blank screen. 'Maybe I can use those graphics as the basis of a game. Played my way, with my rules,' she emphasised with a pointed glance in El's direction. With a growing sense of confidence, she continued. 'You see, I've decided to tell Dad that I'm doing art and computer science when I leave school. But before I start uni, I'm going to go up north to look for Mum.'

She's the only one I can talk to, Callie thought. She's the only one who might understand what's just happened to me and what I might do with that knowledge. She thought of their mother, how she'd abandoned her family to follow her heart. Yes, her mother would understand all right.

'We've just had this conversation, Callie.' El looked impatient. 'You know Dad won't let you go.'

'He can't stop me, and neither can you,' Callie said calmly. 'Once I leave school, I can do what I want.'

'But I don't want you to go!'

Surprised, Callie turned to El. 'Then come with me?' she suggested.

'No. Our mother left us all those years ago. She didn't want us in her life then, so why should she want us now?'

'Things have changed, that's why. We're older, able to look after ourselves. We won't be making any demands on her. I think we should go.'

'What if she wants you to stay with her?' For the first time, El put her fears into words. 'What if she doesn't want me there?'

'Why should she want me to stay and not you?' Callie asked, surprised.

El blinked. 'Because … because …' she stammered.

'Because, because?' Callie mimicked. 'If she wants me, she'll want you too, El. Of course she will. But she might not want either of us. And if that's the case, then at least we'll know where we stand.'

'What about uni?'

'I'm planning to go but I'm going to do the courses I want, whether Dad agrees or not. I'm not going to stay with Mum. I'll come back.'

'Tell that to Dad. I bet he won't believe you.'

'Don't you see? If he lets me go, I'll always come back. But he can't control my life forever.' Callie took a deep breath. 'And neither can you, El.'

Meg felt like cheering. El looked stunned. Then she rested her hand on her sister's shoulder. 'I'll come with you,' she said.

'And we'll both come back, I promise.' Callie smiled. 'In the meantime, you must tell Dad that you're going to do medicine or nursing, or whatever. You're really very good at looking after people.'

'How do you know?'

Callie shrugged. 'I just know, that's all.' She turned to Meg. 'What about you? What are your plans after the HSC?'

'I've been thinking about that.' Meg gazed out the window, not seeing anything as she struggled to find the words to express something she felt she'd always known. 'Music's important to me — as necessary as breathing. I really want to learn all about it, so I'm going to study it full-time when I leave school. And I'm going to ask my olds if I can start having music lessons right now, just to see how I go.' She smiled self-consciously. 'I can make sense of my life through music. And I think I can do some good with it too.'

Callie recognised Meg's words. 'Can you play the lute?' She just had to know.

'Of course not!' Meg pulled a face.

Callie looked at her paintbox. 'You haven't got a lute?'

'No.' Meg shook her head. 'You're still not with it, are you?'

'What's the time? How long was I unconscious?'

'About five minutes. It's a quarter past five.'

Callie did a quick calculation. They'd been in Camelot for nearly three days. A lot had happened in that time. She shook back her shoulders, feeling suddenly cheerful. None of them had been hurt by the experience because none of it was real.

An excited barking caught their attention. The noise

almost drowned the sound of a hesitant knock. El flung the door open and Honey streaked in. She skidded to a halt, stuck a leg into the air and began to scratch vigorously. Meg bent over and grabbed the squirming dog, clutching her tightly as she fondled the silky ears.

'Oh, it's you.' But El didn't sound unfriendly as she stepped aside to let Stephen through the door.

Callie gaped at him. He smiled at her, then held out a notebook organiser to Meg. 'You dropped this on the bus this morning. I found it under my seat after you'd got off, so I thought I'd better return it. Lucky it had your name and address in it. I went next door but there was no reply when I knocked. But then I heard your voices. I'm glad I found you, Meg.'

'Thanks.' Meg put Honey down and took the notebook from Stephen. She frowned at him. 'Have we met before? I mean, before you got on the bus this morning? I feel I sort of know you.'

'We haven't been formally introduced. My name's Stephen.' He nodded to El and Callie as Meg told him their names. 'I feel I sort of know you all too,' he said. 'It's almost as if …' A shrill ring interrupted him. With a grunt of apology, he pulled his mobile out of his pocket.

'Howell? Yeah, of course I remember.'

Callie gasped and tried to hide her shock as Stephen listened.

'No, I can't come over just yet, but I'll see you later. What's your address?'

'Friend of yours?' Callie couldn't help asking as Stephen pocketed the mobile.

'Not really. Not yet.' Stephen was still smiling. 'He's new to the school. His folks have just come out from England and he has to do the HSC. But he's way behind in maths. He asked me to coach him today. I told him to get in touch.'

'Thanks for returning this.' Meg tucked the organiser into her schoolbag.

'I would've got here sooner but there's been a really bad fire. The roads have been blocked off for a while.'

'Fire?' Callie's head jerked up.

'Yeah. At the youth hostel down the street. You know, the one they call The Tower? I just picked up my car, but I was held up coming here. There was a cop directing the traffic. He told me what had happened.'

'Was anyone hurt?' Callie asked quickly.

'I don't think so. The cop said this scruffy teenager raised the alarm and made sure everyone got out safely. But then he just disappeared. They've looked everywhere for him. I guess they thought he might have died in the fire. But no-one's seen him.'

'Lev,' Callie whispered. 'It was Lev.'

'That loser from school that you scanned into the program with …?' Meg's voice faltered as she glanced sideways at Stephen.

Callie nodded, not trusting herself to speak.

'Rubbish!' El said briskly, scratching her arm as she spoke. 'You can't possibly know it was Lev.'

'I can,' said Callie. 'I do. And I know where he's gone. He's back in Camelot, being a knight.'

'You have to be joking!'

'He's brave,' said Callie. 'He's not a loser, he's a hero.'

El shook her head. 'I think you'd better come and lie down.'

Searching for clues to Callie's weird behaviour, Stephen looked to El and Meg for guidance. 'I guess I'd better get going,' he said uncertainly.

'No! Don't go.' Callie couldn't bear to let him leave. He was part of this; he couldn't walk out of their lives now.

'Now that you know where we live, maybe you'll come and see us again?' Meg sent a concerned glance in Callie's direction.

'Yeah, okay. I will.' Stephen looked pleased as he opened the door and stepped out of the workroom. The others followed him out.

'Jeez, these fires are bad.' Meg sniffed the thick, ash-laden air.

'There's a ring of fire all round the city. That's why it took such a long time to bring the fire at the youth hostel under control,' said Stephen. 'The fire brigades are stretched to the limit. I heard on the radio that they're trying to bring in firefighters from other states to help.' He raised a hand in farewell as he strode off up the path. 'See ya!' he called over his shoulder.

A ring of fire around the city. A ring of fire around Camelot. And a loser/hero who crossed time and space to rescue people from a burning tower. Where were they really? What was going on?

'I wish it would start raining.' El fanned herself with one hand. 'It's so bloody hot.' She began to scratch herself again.

'Show me.' Callie grabbed El's arm and inspected the pink rash spattered with dark red spots. 'Fleabites,' she whispered.

'I told you before, Honey needs a bath.'

'I think you'd better go to a doctor. Just in case.'

'For fleabites?' El began to laugh. 'Get real, Callie!'

THE LADY OF SHALOTT

On either side the river lie
Long fields of barley and of rye,
That clothe the wold and meet the sky;
And thro the field the road runs by
   To many-tower'd Camelot;
And up and down the people go,
Gazing where the lilies blow
Round an island there below,
   The island of Shalott.

Willows whiten, aspens quiver,
little breezes dusk and shiver
Thro' the wave that runs for ever
By the island in the river
   Flowing down to Camelot.
Four grey walls, and four grey towers,
Overlook a space of flowers,
And the silent isle imbowers
   The Lady of Shalott.

By the margin, willow-veil'd,
Slide the heavy barges trail'd
By slow horses; and unhail'd
The shallop flitteth silken-sail'd
   Skimming down to Camelot:
But who hath seen her wave her hand?

Or at the casement seen her stand?
Or is she known in all the land,
  The Lady of Shalott?

Only reapers, reaping early
In among the bearded barley,
Hear a song that echoes cheerly
From the river winding clearly,
  Down to tower'd Camelot;
And by the moon the reaper weary,
Piling sheaves in uplands airy,
Listening, whispers 'Tis the fairy
      Lady of Shalott.'

Part II

There she weaves by night and day
A magic web with colours gay.
She has heard a whisper say,
A curse is on her if she stay
  To look down to Camelot.
She knows not what the curse may be,
And so she weaveth steadily,
And little other care hath she,
  The Lady of Shalott.
And moving thro' a mirror clear
That hangs before her all the year,

Shadows of the world appear.
There she sees the highway near
    Winding down to Camelot:
There the river eddy whirls,
And there the surly village-churls,
And the red cloaks of market girls,
    Pass onward from Shalott.

Sometimes a troop of damsels glad,
An abbot on an ambling pad,
Sometimes a curly shepherd lad,
Or long-hair'd page in crimson clad,
    Goes by to tower'd Camelot;
And sometimes thro' the mirror blue
The knights come riding two and two:
She hath no loyal knight and true,
    The Lady of Shalott.

But in her web she still delights
To weave the mirror's magic sights,
For often thro' the silent nights
A funeral, with plumes and with lights,
    And music, went to Camelot:
Or when the moon was overhead,
Came two young lovers lately wed;
'I am half sick of shadows,' said
    The Lady of Shalott.

Part III

A bow-shot from her bower-eaves,
He rode between the barley sheaves,
The sun came dazzling thro' the leaves,
And flam'd upon the brazen greaves
    Of bold Sir Lancelot.
A red-cross knight for ever kneel'd
To a lady in his shield,
That sparkled on the yellow field,
    Beside remote Shalott.

The gemmy bridle glitter'd free,
Like to some branch of stars we see
Hung in the golden Galaxy.
The bridle bells rang merrily
    As he rode down to Camelot:
And from his blazon'd baldric slung
A mighty silver bugle hung,
And as he rode his armour rung,
    Beside remote Shalott.

All in the blue unclouded weather
Thick-jewell'd shone the saddle-leather,
The helmet and the helmet-feather
Burn'd like one burning flame together,
    As he rode down to Camelot.

As often thro' the purple night,
Below the starry clusters bright,
Some bearded meteor, trailing light,
   Moves over still Shalott.

His broad clear brow in sunlight glow'd;
On burnish'd hooves his war-horse trode;
From underneath his helmet flow'd
His coal-black curls as on he rode,
   As he rode down to Camelot.
From the bank and from the river
He flash'd into the crystal mirror,
'Tirra lirra,' by the river
   Sang Sir Lancelot.

She left the web, she left the loom,
She made three paces thro' the room,
She saw the water-lily bloom,
She saw the helmet and the plume,
   She look'd down to Camelot.
Out flew the web and floated wide;
The mirror cracked from side to side;
'The curse is come upon me,' cried
   The Lady of Shalott.

Part IV

In the stormy east-wind straining,
The pale yellow woods were waning,
The broad stream in his banks complaining,
Heavily the low sky raining
  Over tower'd Camelot;
Down she came and found a boat
Beneath a willow left afloat,
And round about the prow she wrote
  The Lady of Shalott.

And down the river's dim expanse —
Like some bold seer in a trance,
Seeing all his own mischance —
With a glassy countenance
  Did she look to Camelot.
And at the closing of the day
She loosed the chain, and down she lay;
The broad stream bore her far away,
  The Lady of Shalott.

Lying, robed in snowy white
That loosely flew to left and right —
The leaves upon her falling light —
Thro' the noises of the night
  She floated down to Camelot:

And as the boat-head wound along
The willowy hills and fields among,
They heard her singing her last song,
   The Lady of Shalott.

Heard a carol, mournful, holy,
Chanted loudly, chanted lowly,
Till her blood was frozen slowly,
And her eyes were darken'd wholly,
   Turn'd to tower'd Camelot.
For ere she reach'd upon the tide
The first house by the water-side,
Singing in her song she died,
   The Lady of Shalott.

Under tower and balcony,
By garden-wall and gallery,
A gleaming shape she floated by,
Dead-pale between the houses high,
   Silent into Camelot.
Out upon the wharfs they came,
Knight and burgher, lord and dame,
And round the prow they read her name,
   The Lady of Shalott.

Who is this? and what is here?
And in the lighted palace near
Died the sound of royal cheer;

And they cross'd themselves with fear,
 All the knights at Camelot:
But Lancelot mused a little space;
He said, 'She has a lovely face;
God in his mercy lend her grace,
 The Lady of Shalott.'

Alfred Lord Tennyson

AUTHOR'S NOTES ON 'SHALOTT'

The legend of The Lady of Shalott is embedded in a story that had its genesis in the Dark Ages, when Welsh bards first sang of a brave and noble king. There are several versions of the Arthurian legend, but the most common is based on Sir Thomas Malory's *Le Morte D'Arthur* (completed 1469-70), which drew together both English and French versions of the story, and became a best-seller thanks to the invention of the printing press.

The story begins with Uther Pendragon, King of all England, who lusts after Igraine, wife of Gorlois, the Duke of Cornwall. Through the trickery of the magician Merlin, Uther takes on the likeness of Gorlois and lies with Igraine, at which time Arthur is conceived. Following the death of Gorlois in battle, Uther subsequently marries Igraine, but the price of Merlin's trickery is to give up Arthur to the magician's care.

Arthur is brought up in Sir Ector's household, his true heritage not known until the time when he succeeds in pulling the sword Excalibur from the stone, so proving that he is the true born king of all Britain.

Arthur's task is to unite the Celtic tribes against Saxon marauders and there are many battles. (Whether Arthur was 'real' or not, early Welsh annals record that there was peace in Britain for several decades in the sixth century, lasting from the Battle of Badon, Arthur's last deciding battle against the Saxons, to the Battle of Camlann at which 'Arthur and Medraut fell'.)

Mordred (Medraut) is conceived when, unknowingly, Arthur sleeps with his half-sister, sometimes called Morgause, wife of King Lot of the Orkneys. Other stories name Mordred's mother as Morgan le Fay, the enchantress, whose magic and ambition for Mordred do so much to harm King Arthur and his realm.

Legend says that Arthur established his court at Camelot; that he married Guinevere, and that he and his knights held court and decided affairs of state seated at a Round Table. One of the knights is Lancelot du Lac of Brittany. He and Guinevere fall in love when Guinevere is captured by one of Arthur's rivals and Lancelot is sent to rescue her. There are many stories of the affair between Lancelot and Guinevere, their quarrels and their partings.

During Lancelot's several absences from court, he meets two young women — although in some versions of the story, they become the same. The first is Elaine of Corbin, daughter of the Fisher King, King Pelles, who tricks Lancelot into her bed when she assumes the disguise of Guinevere. As a result, the most perfect knight of all the realm, Galahad, is born. It is Galahad who is deemed pure and worthy enough to succeed in finding the Holy Grail, to heal the Waste Land and cure the Fisher King of his wounds. In some versions of the story, Lancelot and Elaine live together for a while, but Lancelot cannot forget Guinevere. Eventually he returns to court, and Elaine dies.

The second young woman is 'the Lily Maid', Elaine of Astolat, on whom Tennyson's poem 'The Lady of Shalott' is based. Banished by Guinevere, Lancelot rides to Astolat in disguise, and takes shelter with a local baron. The baron's daughter, Elaine, falls in love with Lancelot, and begs him to wear her favour (the red sleeve of her gown) in his helmet when he goes to the 9th diamond joust at Winchester. He fights incognito, and wins. Elaine begs Lancelot to marry her, or even live with her, but he rejects her advances. Heartbroken, she lies down in a boat and dies. Her brother, Sir Lavaine, takes her body down to Camelot, and Lancelot is stricken with remorse when he realises what has happened.

Following the French tradition, much of the legend is taken up with the romantic affairs of the court. Tristan and Isolde is another famous love story, while the marriage of Sir Gawain and Ragnall, the 'Loathly Lady' gives a touch of magic and the supernatural to courtly affairs.

In fact, pagan magic often mixes with Christianity in the story. Merlin, Morgan le Fay and Nimue all weave spells. There are battles against supernatural creatures like the Questing Beast and the Green Knight (who, when his head is lopped off by Gawain, picks it up and replaces it.) But the greatest adventure of all is when the knights leave court in search of the Holy Grail, a quest at which only Galahad, Bors and Perceval are successful.

Thanks to Mordred, the liaison between Guinevere and Lancelot becomes known. Guinevere is to be burned at the stake, but Lancelot rescues her and many knights die in the battle that follows. Lancelot leaves the court and, in Arthur's absence, Mordred unites the younger knights in a bid to win both the kingdom and the love of Guinevere for himself.

Arthur returns and he and Mordred meet at Camlann to discuss a treaty. A soldier draws his sword to kill an adder and, mistaking the signal, the soldiers begin the battle at which both Arthur and Mordred are mortally wounded. On his deathbed, Arthur commands his loyal knight, Sir Bedivere, to cast Excalibur into the lake.

Repenting of their role in the downfall of Camelot, Lancelot and Guinevere spend the rest of their days apart, Lancelot in a hermitage and Guinevere living as a nun in Almesbury.

Knights, ladies, the Holy Grail, The Lady of Shalott and all the romance of the court of King Arthur are subjects close to the heart of Sydney author Felicity Pulman. She's so intrigued by the scenes and characters of this by-gone age that she has written short stories and given talks about it, and even taken photographs of well-known Arthurian sites in Britain.

The books she has published include *Ghost Boy*, *Wally the Waterdragon* and *Surfing the Future*. *Shalott* is Felicity's first novel for Random House.